A Place To Call
Home...

By Marion Siebert Jensen

Dedication

Dedicated to the memory of wise, courageous Mennonite people

*They risked the unknown to escape oppression, ultimately
providing their descendants with a future of religious freedom.*

Acknowlegements

My heartfelt thanks to my daughter, who helped prepare this
work for publication, and to my daughter-in-law, whose
computer support enabled me to write this story

Prologue

Holland, 1600

In the early 1600's, after Martin Luther had broken the grasp the Catholic Church had had on the civilized world, many reformers appeared on the scene. Among them was Menno Simon. He preached that the Bible was the ultimate authority and to be honored above man's preaching. The greatest difference between him and other reformers was that he believed all wars were futile, and that, although citizens should be loyal to their country, they should refuse to bear arms under any circumstance. Those who followed his teachings came to be called Mennonites.

This brought about some persecution, and some of the men were imprisoned for this stand. But the troublesome Mennonites stood together, and King Frederick realized he could not imprison all of them. Besides, they were useful to him. They had taken useless swampland and made it profitable, thus adding to the economy of Holland. The king remembered a group from England that had come for asylum when they had been persecuted by the Papists. They had, however, not stayed in Holland long once they heard about religious freedom in the New World. Perhaps these Mennonite people would leave, too, after they had developed the land to be profitable.

Meanwhile, he would leave the Mennonites alone but take a king's portion of their crops to feed his army. He cared little for all these religious matters. His motto was "Live and let live," unless doing so interfered too greatly with his purpose. These new religions seemed only to bring about greater conflict.

****

Prussia, 1680

Meanwhile, the king of Germany had seen the industrious Mennonites retrieve useless swampland and make it productive. He could use them in the area along the Vistula River. The king had recently acquired this useless land through his latest conquest. While the land gave him greater access to waterways, it might as well be productive farmland. So he invited the Mennonites to migrate to this area. He promised them exemption from the military, but he reserved the right to rescind that privilege later, after the land was made productive. The Mennonites accepted his kind invitation, expecting him to be true to his word and not understanding that he might, at some point, change his mind. The king kept his promise until the citizens living nearby grumbled that these newcomers were getting special privileges. The Mennonites were in a quandary. They did not want to cause trouble, but neither would they compromise their stand about military service. They gathered together to pray that God would give them direction.

****

Russia, 1700

When the news came that the Czar of Russia was about to be married to the German Princess Catherine, the Mennonites hoped that she would champion their cause. She had on previous occasions indicated respect for this strange group of believers who lived so frugally and were such productive farmers. She herself was opposed to war, having lost family members in various conflicts. Maybe she would persuade the Czar to be content with his holdings after his latest acquisition between the Volga and the Yushanee rivers. After acquiring this huge area of land, the Czar could not persuade citizens to occupy this area because of the frequent flooding. It was thought that this land was useless.

Catherine knew the history of the Mennonites. She knew they had made wetlands in Holland productive, and that they had made the arduous move to the Vistula area. Perhaps the Czar could persuade these people to migrate again. She persuaded her husband to send emissaries to investigate the matter. She informed him of their adversity to military service. Even with that knowledge, he thought it worthwhile and sent his most persuasive agents, relaying again to the Mennonites the promise that they would not have to serve in the military. Additionally, he gave them the right to set up schools in their own language (the Low German), and he promised they could brew and sell their own beer.

These promises proved to be quite persuasive, and the Mennonite group accepted the invitation after they had sent representatives to inspect the land offered. They were, after all, an adventurous group and often compared themselves to the wandering Jewish people. When they felt God leading them, they followed, even though some were reluctant to leave their comfortable, established homes and villages. They all owned sturdy wagons and horses, and roads had been established so the move would be comparatively easy. They did not expect trouble from the Russian citizens, because no one would want that swamp. At last they would be free to establish their own communities. They could keep their language and their schools and be a community to themselves.

The women felt the hardships of this move, since they had to pack up all their household goods. Also, because they were limited in space on the wagons, they had to leave many things behind. They worked hard to pack their special heirlooms and the items that would be essential to keeping house in their new location. The trip itself was wearisome. It took many days to make the trip, and without cushions on the hard wagon seats, they felt aches in muscles they hadn't even realized they had. They also had the difficult job of caring for the children, who sometimes complained about the rocks on the road hurting their feet and other discomforts of the trail. The camping at night was not conducive to comfortable sleeping. There was always the threat of robbers, so most of the men slept "with one eye open," as they tried to protect their women and children as well as their property and the animals they were taking with them. It made quite a caravan!

Chapter One

Katharina Epp glanced toward the barn as she hung the dishpan on the nail outside the kitchen door of her modest home along the Volga River. She wondered why her husband's brother was here again talking to Hoinz. It seemed he came too often, and this usually led to an argument about something. Cornelius was Hoinz' older brother, and he felt that, as the older brother, he could give advice to Hoinz, whether Hoinz wanted it or needed it or not. Katharina wondered what it was about this time.

There had been some anxiety in their close-knit community ever since the Czarina Catherine had died. The Mennonites were anxious to see if the Czar would keep the promises that Catherine had made them. So far, little had changed since her death, and the Mennonites settled back into their comfortable lifestyle. She remembered well the stories her grandparents had told of coming to this area at Catherine's invitation. The move had been difficult, and, during the first few years, they had suffered many hardships. It took several years of hard work to make the swampy land productive. But for the last hundred years, they had lived very comfortably. They had their own schools, their own land, their own language, and, for the most part, nothing to do with the surrounding Russian people. Some of the Mennonites had learned to speak a bit of Russian. It was helpful when they had dealings with the government officials who came around at harvest time to collect the taxes on the crops they had raised. Katharina was content, and she hoped that things would never change.

She had a large garden which helped to feed her eleven children. Their cows produced enough milk and the hens laid more than enough eggs to feed the family. The extra could be bartered for salt and sugar at their local store. The children helped with all the work.

She brushed a tear from her eye as she looked toward the old oak tree behind the house where two markers reminded her of the baby boy who had died just ten days after he was born, and of daughter Lieska, who had fallen from the second story barn door and broken her neck when she was just ten years old. Even though she had nine healthy children, she still felt the loss of these two. It often seemed like just a day ago that they had dug those graves and placed those precious bodies there. Now, at age fifty, she knew her childbearing years were over. Perhaps it would not be long before Sarah and Cornelius, the two oldest, would each marry, and she would have grandchildren. Her arms often ached to hold a tiny baby falling asleep on her shoulder as she rocked it on the rocking chair that her grandmother had insisted on bringing from the Danzig area.

Hoinz had been looking for additional land in anticipation of his sons and daughters setting up their own farming operations. But land was hard to come by. The government had sold them the area between the Volga and the Ural Rivers for restoration, and that area was now populated with Mennonites who had come from Prussia. The government had refused their requests to expand to other areas.

Katharina forced her mind back to the present. She had better get supper started. She surely hoped her husband's brother Cornelius wouldn't stay for supper. She didn't want to hear the argument continued at the table. Whatever they were arguing about, the children didn't need to hear it. And the older children would be tempted to enter into the conversation, which would only lead to noise and confusion. She liked quiet mealtimes, with only soft requests for someone to pass some food item from the other end of the table.

Katie had already peeled the potatoes and Maria was setting the table when Katharina reentered her spacious kitchen. Margaret was placing the silverware with Maria's instruction. Milk would be brought from the spring house after the men came in. Katharina was proud of her daughters. They were a great help with the housework and the cooking. Even now her girls were busy preparing their evening meal, which most often consisted of fried potatoes with eggs, some sauerkraut, and maybe canned applesauce or *Plautz*[1].

She called to her two youngest, who were busy kicking a clod of dirt around the barnyard. "Peter, William: You need to come wash your hands and face. Sarah and Cornelius have already finished the milking, and Father will soon come in."

She saw Johann come around the corner of the house with a basket of eggs. "How many eggs did you get today?" she asked. Not waiting for an answer, she continued, "Did you give the hens plenty of feed and make sure they had enough water? We must feed them well so they will continue to lay through the winter."

"Yes, Mother, there is enough to make them lay and get fat as well. I hope you will make chicken noodle soup soon. And I know just which hen to cook. She always pecks at me when I reach for the eggs under her. I would like to see her head chopped off and her put into the kettle."

---

[1] a pastry made of flattened bread dough and a fruit sauce topping

"Now, now, that is no way to talk. We must be kind and take good care of our animals. I know which hen you mean. She is feisty, I know, but she is one of our best layers. We will not cook a hen that lays an egg almost every day."

"I know, but sometimes I think the animals should be kind to us, too!"

Fortunately, Hoinz's brother Cornelius climbed into his wagon, clucked to his horses, and started for home. Hoinz came toward the house, and Katharina was curious to know what the visit had been about, but she knew better than to ask. Her husband would tell her all about it when the time was right. Right now was the time to think about supper. With a good deal of sputtering and splashing, Father and the older boys washed the dirt and grime of their afternoon's work from their hands and faces. Katharina was always happy when the spring weather warmed up enough to move this bit of action to the back porch. It allowed the family greater freedom to splash about to cool the heat from their bodies, and it certainly helped to keep her kitchen floor clean. The family was soon gathered around the large table. From habit they all quietly bowed their heads waiting for Father to ask God's blessing on the food.

The usually short prayer was a little longer tonight. And Maria sneaked a look at her brother, Abraham. She caught him looking at her as well and detected the slight wink he gave her. This could only mean that he knew something that she didn't, but he would explain it later. Meanwhile, she wondered why her father was asking God for direction in all their plans. He never did that at the supper table. It was the sort of request he might make at bedtime prayers, but not at the supper table. Something must be up. Maria wondered if it had anything to do with Uncle Cornelius' visit that afternoon.

When the prayer ended, the food was passed around, starting with Father, of course. They all ate heartily, for they had all worked hard all day with the necessary farm work. Sarah and Cornelius had helped their father put up hay. Katie had helped her mother around the house, while Maria and Margaret had herded the six cows along the road where free foliage was found for them to feed. Abraham had been responsible for cleaning the second story of the barn in preparation for the hay that would be stored there when winter came.

The conversation picked up after the first pangs of hunger had been satisfied, but even before that, Maria spoke softly to her mother. "Do I have to eat this sauerkraut? I don't like the taste, and it always gives me a stomach-ache."

Before her mother could reply, Father said sternly, "Eat what is on your plate. Be thankful for what the Lord has provided, and it won't upset your stomach." Maria tried to be thankful, but she almost gagged as she dutifully took another spoonful of the awful stuff. Mother looked at her sympathetically, but they both knew there was nothing to be done about it. What Father said was the rule, and Maria had to abide by it. Even when Abraham tried to take a spoonful from her plate, Father gave him a warning look, and he resisted. Maria finally managed to finish what was on her plate. With great relief she helped herself to the *Plautz* as it was passed around.

Now Peter complained, "William always takes the biggest piece of *Plautz*. Why can't I have the bigger piece just once?"

This time Father looked at Peter and spoke up harshly. "Let's have some peace and quiet at the table. Peter, you don't look like you are starving, and the pieces of *Plautz* look the same size to me."

Then Father looked at the other children and asked about the garden and whether the beet tops would soon be ready for *Borscht*.[2] Mother replied that she thought it would be only a few more days. The rhubarb looked good, and she planned to cook some sauce the next day. Abraham reported that he had checked the mulberry trees behind the barn, and some of the berries showed a little red. If the weather continued warm they would soon be ready to eat.

The younger children all smacked their lips in anticipation of mulberries and cream for supper.

Father continued, "I walked through the wheat field. It should be ready for cutting next week. The barley and oats also look good. We will be very busy for the next month or two." He gave a knowing look to the older children. "If and when we get the harvesting done, we should have time for some relaxing and visiting with the neighbors and relatives who live nearby. My brother Cornelius asked if we could help him with his harvest. His boys are too young to be of much use. He would, in turn, help with the threshing. I think it is about time his kids learn to help with the farm work, but he thinks they are too young, and, of course, Tante Graetcha indulges those kids too much."

Mother Katharina thought to herself, "So that is what the visit was about. I'm relieved."

After supper the family scattered, all having things to do before nightfall. As Maria stepped out of the back door to throw out the dishwater, Abraham gave a low whistle from the barn door. Quickly, she walked toward him, knowing he had something to tell her. Maria felt closest to her brother Abraham. They had much in common, as

---

[2] beet soup

they were both adventuresome. Whenever they had free time, they would wander down to the river and watch for schools of fish or catch tadpoles to see if their land legs were beginning to grow. They studied the plants along the river and often chewed on the ends of the long-stemmed grasses.

Now Abraham had some fascinating information that he wanted to share with Maria. "You know, Karl came by this afternoon while I was cleaning the hayloft. He told me the church elders had come to see his father and had discussed making a trip to America to see if the stories they heard about that land are true. They spoke as though our people might consider moving to America, for there is unlimited land available. They said that the 'handwriting was on the wall': that the Russian government was tightening the rules for the Mennonites, not letting us buy additional land, and no doubt the military exemption will soon be retracted. They said it was time to think about the future."

"Oh, my," Maria replied. "Isn't that exciting? Wouldn't it be great to see the ocean? I can't imagine what it would be like to see only water in every direction. I remember Mother telling stories that her grandmother had told of the big ships that used to come to the port in Prussia when she was a little girl. Do you think our parents would ever move from this land along the Volga?"

"I don't know, Maria, but I think it would be grand! They say New York City has buildings taller than our windmill and thousands of people with fancy buggies and carriages pulled by fancy horses. I wish we had something better than old Prince and Queen. But you know our parents. They would never have anything fancy, lest it make us proud. Now don't go telling this to anyone, or I'll get into trouble. You know how Father doesn't want me talking to friends when I have work to do."

Maria agreed to keep the secret, and the brother and sister walked quietly back to the house. They stopped at the back porch where the other children had already washed their feet in preparation for bedtime. Abraham couldn't resist flicking a little water at his sister, and the two were soon engaged in a limited water fight, until Margaret came to the door to call them in for family prayers. The family was waiting, for tomorrow would be another long day of hard work for all.

The family had gathered in the great room where Father now held the Bible for the traditional evening reading and prayers. After checking with the children to see if all the farm animals had been securely locked up, he turned to the scriptures, reading from Psalms 16. When he came to verse eleven, Maria wondered if there was a special reason he had chosen this portion. "Thou wilt shew me the path of life: in thy presence *is* fulness of joy; at thy right hand there are pleasures for evermore." And then he prayed for each of his children, that they would always seek to honor the Lord and live in humility and peace. He prayed for the Czar and others that were in the government, that they would look kindly on the Mennonite people, remembering how the useless land had been made profitable for the country. He prayed that there would be peace in all the world, and that people and countries would be content with what they had; that all wars would cease, and that God would give wisdom to the church leaders as well.

After this, everyone was ready to go to bed.

Chapter Two

Maria crawled into bed beside her sister Margaret, whose deep breathing soon indicated she had gone to sleep. But sleep would not come to Maria. She kept thinking about what Abraham had told her. Could it be possible that some of her people would travel to that far-off place called America? In one breath she wished she could go with them, and quickly another thought took over. They would never return. Such a trip was too risky. They would shipwreck, or sea monsters would eat them, or perhaps the heathens that were called Indians would chop their heads off. But apparently some people had made the trip, for Mr. Nuefeldt had received a letter from someone in America and it sounded as though they were prospering in that far-off land.

And then just as she was about to drop off to sleep, she heard the voice of her father just on the other side of her bedroom wall.

"Cornelius had other things on his mind while he was here today. The elders of our church visited him yesterday. Elder Nuefeldt had had a letter from his cousin. You know those people that migrated to America two years ago when they couldn't find land to buy here nearby? They seem to be doing well, and they are encouraging us to migrate, too. Elder Nuefeldt, Elder Fast, and Elder Jantzen want to have a meeting at the church tomorrow night about the feasibility of such an undertaking. I have so much to do, with harvesting coming on, but I suppose I'd better attend so I will at least know what is going on."

Then she heard her mother reply quite loudly, "What a crazy idea! I am totally opposed to it. Why do our people always want to move to some far-off place? Why can't we be satisfied where we are?"

Her father retorted, "Well, do you want your sons to go off to war and maybe get killed? And besides, we cannot buy more land. If our children get married, as two of them probably will soon, how will they live? This farm cannot produce enough to support us plus nine other families."

Maria couldn't hear her mother's reply to this, and she felt guilty for having heard what she had. It was a sin to eavesdrop, and she quickly asked God to forgive her, although she couldn't have helped hearing what had been said. No doubt her parents had assumed everyone else was asleep. The older children slept upstairs, but Maria and Margaret had the room next to their parents, and the walls were not a good sound barrier.

The conversation had ended, but Maria kept putting two and two together. She was sure there was a connection between what her parents had said and what Abraham had reported from his conversation with Karl.

Mother had to call her three times in the morning, for when she finally fell asleep, she had had vivid dreams of traveling across the ocean and finding herself flying through the air headed for the moon.

She looked disheveled and half awake at the breakfast table and was unwilling to talk to anyone. Finally her mother felt her forehead to see if she had a fever. But Father told her to shape up because there was much work to do. She made a gallant effort to look awake, and, after eating some mush and drinking some cold milk, she did feel better.

But how could she keep this secret? She dared not tell even Abraham, because that would show she had eavesdropped. She felt that, if she didn't tell someone, she would burst with excitement. Maybe she could tell her pet sheep, for today she would be required to watch the sheep as they fed in the hayfield that the men had harvested yesterday. She hoped telling it even to a sheep who could not understand would ease the pressure building in her head and in her heart.

At the dinner table at noon Father announced that he had been called to attend a meeting at the church that evening, so the family would have to take on added responsibilities for the afternoon's work. No one dared ask him what the meeting was about. Abraham cast a knowing look toward Maria, and she almost choked on the *Ruggabrot*[3] she had just bitten into.

That afternoon, as Maria was watching the sheep, she again thought about the strange things that were going on in their community. Would they be leaving everything they had ever known to go to a place so far away? But then old Jezebel, the leader in their flock of sheep, started toward the wheat field, and Maria ran to head her off before all the sheep could follow and trample the grain that was about to be harvested. Jezebel faced her defiantly, but when Maria whacked her on the head with her stick, she obediently turned back to the hayfield where the grazing was less lucrative. Maria was thankful that the problem had been averted. She knew the consequences if the sheep trampled the wheat, even if it was a small area.

---

[3] rye bread

Later in the afternoon Abraham brought her a jug of water and a bit of bread with a little jam on it. He had finished cleaning the haymow and had a few minutes before he needed to start the evening chores.

"What do you think the meeting at the church is about?" he asked.

"You know it must be about the men going to explore the possibility of migrating to America," Maria replied. "It sounds exciting to me, but I just don't think it will ever happen. Our people have lived in this area for a hundred years. How could we possibly move all our stuff that far?" She dared not reveal her knowledge of the parental conversation she had overheard.

Abraham assured her that there was a good possibility that it might happen and then hurried back to the farmyard, lest he be found loitering in the middle of the day.

Maria kept close watch over the sheep the rest of the afternoon, and then it was time for them to head back to their pen where she would pump water into their drinking trough. Her pet lamb kept close to her side as she moved from one side of the flock to the other to keep them moving toward the farmyard. She loved working with the sheep, even if old Jezebel often challenged her. Tending the sheep was a lot more fun than weeding the garden or picking the peas or beans as they became ready to harvest. After securely penning the sheep and filling their trough with fresh water, she made her way toward the house.

William and Peter met her in the house yard. "Did you get along with Jezebel today?" they asked, almost in unison.

She replied, "We had just one little argument, but my stick and I won." And then she remembered, "I forgot to take water to The Czar." And she turned to complete her duties. Father kept the ram of the flock locked up because he might harm someone. The children referred to the ram as The Czar, but not so the parents would hear. Even though the Mennonites were not fond of their national ruler, they knew they had to pay proper respect to those in authority over them.

Father was bringing the horses into the farmyard just as Maria finished. He was home early because of the church meeting. After leading the horses to the stock tank to drink, he took them into the barn and removed their harnesses. He asked Maria to feed the horses while he hurried to the house to eat an early supper and walk the short distance to the church. He ate hurriedly and then walked to the bedroom to change from his dirty work clothes to clean ones.

Katharina followed him and suggested he wear his Sunday clothes to the meeting, but he replied brusquely, "This is not a church meeting, and this clean shirt and pants will do."

Katharina knew her husband was upset at all the goings on, and she wished she could be of some comfort to him. But all she could think to reply was, "I'll pray the meeting goes well."

She appreciated the look he gave her as he laid his hand on her shoulder. "Let's just pray the Lord leads us." And he walked out the door.

When Hoinz arrived at the meeting house, he saw that several neighbors were already gathered. Pastor Epp was at the door and warmly greeted everyone. At seven o'clock the doors were closed, and Pastor Epp took his place behind the pulpit. Hoinz glanced toward the front of the room and saw Elders Nuefeldt, Fast, and Jantzen sitting on the front bench. Pastor Epp motioned for all to stand. He called them to prayer. He intoned God for guidance, faith, a sense of unity on the men gathered there, and wisdom for any and all decisions made. In his most ministerial voice he finished, "In the name of Your most Holy Son, *Aaammmen*."

Then he turned the meeting over to Elder Nuefeldt, who stood and addressed those in attendance. "My dear brethren in Christ Jesus, I have this past week received a letter from our brother, my cousin William Nuefeldt. You will remember that he, with about seventy other households, took the courageous trip to settle in the New World, also called America. They arrived there safely, although not without some adversity, as Brother Abrams died before they arrived at their destination. After they were well settled, a sickness came to their community, and Mrs. Nuefeldt, as well as three children in the group, died from this illness. But the community is now prospering, and they would like us to consider sending a group to join them. They need both young men and women for their sons and daughters to marry and enlarge their group. There is plenty of rich, fertile farm ground available. The government is very cooperative and is offering land at an unheard-of advantage. The railroad is seeking settlers that would develop the land; of course, they wish to see their business profit from those who would be shipping farm crops and animals to the populated areas further east. He says it does get somewhat lonesome at times, since they are few in number, and they do not wish to be assimilated into the English-speaking people around them."

Mr. Nuefeldt turned to Mr. Fast, who now stood and addressed the men, who were beginning to become restless. They had worked hard all day and knew that longer days of hard work in the harvest lay ahead of them. "We would like you to consider this move. We know it will not be without some loss and hardship, but you see what is going on around us. There is no more land available for us here, and the rumors we get from Petersburg are not encouraging. How long before the Czar will take our young men to be killed as he adds to his kingdom?" And Mr. Fast sat down beside Mr. Nuefeldt, nodding to Mr. Jantzen to take the floor.

"We feel that this letter that Brother Nuefeldt has received does not give us enough information, although it is an encouraging start. We suggest that we send a delegation to further investigate this matter, and that we then make a unified decision. Are there any questions?"

Hoinz' brother Cornelius was the first to stand. "How much will all this cost? There are some here who could well afford whatever, but we also have those who, through no fault of their own, are experiencing financial hardships. Will they be left behind to fend for themselves against the power of the Czar?"

"That is a debatable question, but I think it should be left unanswered until a later date," was Elder Nuefeldt's reply. "We just want to get a feel for your ideas. Do you think this is something we should pursue?"

Mr. Regier stood and commented, "I think this whole thing is absurd. Just because there is a rumor that our men will be taken into the military, you act like it is the end of the world. Why is it that our people always want to pull up stakes and move when a little adversity comes along? They moved from Holland to Prussia at great expense, then from Prussia to our present location. If we settle in America, in due time, that government will also want our men for the military. Where will we go then? If I know my geography, there is no other continent on the globe. Will we then attempt a settlement on the moon? Sometimes I think we should try to fit into the country and assimilate. The Czar in all his speeches talks only of peace and prosperity. I move we forget the whole thing."

Now Pastor Epp stood and quieted the crowd, who were becoming a bit unruly. "This meeting was not called to make any decision. The elders have made their case. We will adjourn in a few minutes. I request that you consider what has been said, and that we meet again next week. That will be the time to make decisions one way or another." Then he took out his Bible, turned to Proverbs 11:13-14, and read, " 'A talebearer revealeth secrets: but he that is of a faithful spirit concealeth the matter. Where no counsel is, th^e people fall: but in the multitude of counsellors there is safety.' Let us pray." He knelt this time beside the pulpit chair and earnestly prayed for wisdom for each of the men to be true to their faith and to earnestly seek wisdom from God in all their affairs. Rising, he dismissed the men, wishing them health and safety as they harvested the bountiful crop the Lord had given them.

The men left quietly, each one engrossed in his own thoughts: thoughts of the urgent harvest, thoughts of the migration, and, for most of them, thoughts of how their wives would react to these developments.

The next day Maria was watching the sheep, making sure they did not stray into the wheat field nearby. Nothing had been said about the meeting at the church the previous evening. Maria was full of curiosity, but when she hinted her interest to her mother, she had been told that it was none of her business and she should concentrate on her chores for the day. This, of course, only served to increase her interest. The sheep were peacefully grazing in the hayfield and Maria was almost dozing when something tickled her ear. Thinking it was a pesky horsefly she swiped at it with her hand only to have her hand grabbed. As she turned she saw Karl Regier laughing at her.

"I caught you sleeping. What would your father say if you were caught sleeping and the sheep got into the wheat field? I'll bet that would give you big trouble." And he continued to grin at her discomfort.

"What are you doing here? Aren't you supposed to be tending your own sheep?"

"No. They are penned up. The shearers are coming this afternoon. I am on my way to Tante Tien's. Mother needs some rhubarb to cook with the mulberries. It is too far for Sis to go, so she sent me. Is your brother Abraham around?"

"He is in the back oat field. Father sent him there to pull out the tall weeds so they won't interfere with his scything next week."

Karl seemed in no hurry to continue his errand. After a moment or two he looked at Maria and said, "Did your father say anything about the meeting last night?"

"No. Did yours?"

"Yes. He said it was a cockeyed idea by Nuefeldt, Jantzen, and Fast to move all Mennonites to a place in America called Nebraska. My father is totally opposed to it. And since we were able to buy the land when the Alfred Nuefeldts left two years ago, we have enough land here to keep us busy for years to come. He thinks those that are always talking about the threats of broken promises from Petersburg are just worrywarts. He says we will stay right here in Russia where we belong." Then he gave her a strange look and continued. "I wish we would go. I like adventure. My grandmother told of how her parents had lived near the water in Prussia and how she loved to see the big ships come into the harbor."

Maria replied, "I don't know if I would like to go, but Father spoke to Mother about it the other night. They thought I was sleeping.

He was talking about the need for additional land and also the threat that my brothers Cornelius and Abraham would have to serve in the Czar's army. My mom doesn't want to leave our home here."

"Well, I'd better get that rhubarb or I'll be in trouble," said Karl as he took off running.

Chapter Three

Over the next few weeks, everyone was very busy from dawn to dusk. There was so much work to do. The harvesting of the oats, wheat, and rye occupied every man in the community, and there was competition to see who would finish first. Father was busy cutting the grain with his scythe. It had to be done just so, so that the grain would fall into the cradle attached to the scythe in smooth order. Each swing of the scythe would make one bundle. Katie and Johann followed Father. They gathered the swath, and, using a few strands of straw, tied it into bundles. Then they stood the bundles upright in groups of eight or ten so that the heads of grain could dry completely. Later these bundles were hauled close to the barn, where they would be stacked twenty to thirty feet high.

After all the grain had been stacked this way, the threshing floor was made ready. It was a flat circular area of hard ground, slightly sloped toward the middle. In late September and early October the grain was spread on this floor and a rolling rock pulled over it by one horse, crushing the heads of straw and grain to make the seeds come out. One or two men with pitchforks would pick up the grain and throw it in the air. The wind would blow the straw and the chaff away, letting the grain fall to the floor. The grain was then carefully sacked. The straw was raked together and stacked for bedding for the animals through the winter, except for the rye straw, which was used to repair the roof of the house and barn. Those who were adept at weaving it together could make a roof that would not leak in any rainstorm. When all the grain had been treated in this labor-intensive way, the harvest was declared over, and the farmers breathed a sigh of relief. Now they could relax, to a degree, until the planting was started the next spring.

Meanwhile, the ladies, if they were not required to help the men in some way, were busy with their own harvesting of garden produce. Every farm had an area near the house that had been slightly excavated. Here cabbages, potatoes, squash, and rutabagas, as well as parsnips, were stored. Layers of straw would be pitched over this produce to keep it from freezing. Dirt was piled over the straw-covered vegetables. In this unique way, the family usually had fresh produce until after Christmas.

The children, too, were busy. They picked wild plums and the grapes near the house in season. Mothers and aunts usually worked together, setting up the quilting frame in the sun. An old sheet was tacked around it. After the fruit had been washed, it was spread on this sheet. Sometimes another sheet was placed over the fruit to protect it from flies. Other times children were given the job of shooing the flies and birds away. If they had hot summer days, the fruit would dry in a few days. If rains came, the operation was moved to the haymow, which had not yet been filled for winter use.

The children ate their fill of fruit as they picked, but they anticipated cookies filled with raisins, as well as the *Plumamos*[4] Mother would make through the winter.

---

[4] *Plumenmoos*, fruit soup

But the meeting at the church was not forgotten. Most of the men took time to attend. Mr. Regier, however, was absent. He had made it clear to everyone that he and his family would not be interested in this crazy project. The others showed reserved interest, but agreed it would be a good idea to send Elders Nuefeldt, Fast, and Jantzen to explore the possibilities of immigrating. They would leave right after the harvesting was over and possibly be back in time for the spring planting. The rest of the community would make sure that their families were taken care of through the winter.

The commissioning service came in late September. Pastor Epp preached on Joshua 1, emphasizing the need to trust in the Lord and to obey all His commands, for they surely had not walked this way before. He cautioned the committee to seek God's guidance in every step and then challenged them to be strong and courageous. He prayed, laying his hands on Elders Nuefeldt, Fast, and Jantzen, in turn, that they would be safe, healthy, and diligent in the commission that was bestowed on them. After the service, many people shook their hands and wished them well. Katharina and many of the other women sought to console the elders' wives, each one thinking of the dangers these men would face. They also realized the loneliness the wives would feel through the coming winter, as well as the very real possibility that the husbands would never return.

All too soon a month had passed, and though the pastor prayed at every service for the departed trio, nothing much was said about the immigration. News came from Petersburg that the government needed additional troops to resist the Turks, who were trying to regain possession of the land the Mennonites now occupied, since it had now become productive farmland. The community would be expected to provide two hundred horses and men, as well as fifty wagons of wheat to provide for their food. An emissary was sent with the horses and the wheat, reminding the government of their military exemption. He returned with the promise that they would not have to serve, but that they needed to send a huge sum of money if they expected to retain this exemption. The Mennonites could maintain their exemption, but they would have to pay the wages for those who took their place. Reluctantly, the congregation took up a collection to satisfy the Czar's ever-increasing demands. This reinforced the determination for many to move, if at all possible, to the new country, named Nebraska.

The students at school, whose schedule had resumed a week after the harvest was finished, often spoke of their dreams of moving to this new land. Those who were opposed to the move were a minority. Karl and a few others dared not speak about their desire to go, because if word of their comments reached their parents, they would be severely punished. They should not disagree with their parents' decision.

At a church service in early November, Pastor Epp announced that the singing school would begin that very afternoon. All those interested were to return to the church by two o'clock. They would sing until four o'clock, giving everyone time to go home, do the chores, and be back for the evening service. All the young people were happy with this announcement, for it gave them an opportunity to socialize.

Maria and Abraham were especially excited, for this was the first year they would be old enough to participate. They spoke of it in subdued tones on their way home from church. "I wonder how many there will be at the singing?" Maria said to her older sister, Katie.

Katie replied, "There should be a large group, because only six of those that were there last year won't be coming this year. Nick and Anna, Abe and Martha, and Will and Alvina got married, so they won't be there. There are a lot of younger people that will be eligible this year."

Maria was wondering if Karl and his sister Matilda would come, but she dare not ask, for fear she would be teased. Her siblings already thought she was sweet on Karl and often teased her about him.

She was happy to see her friend Matilda as soon as she returned to the church with her older siblings. She whispered to Matilda her pleasure at seeing her, and Matilda whispered back that Karl had hoped she would be there. Maria glanced toward the group of younger boys that had assembled and saw Karl looking directly at her. Blushing, she hastily looked down at the ground and tried to straighten her skirt as though it had been ruffled in the wind.

Elder Ziebet tapped his baton on the bench near him, and the group quietly came to order. He announced his general plans for the next few months, emphasizing that they would be expected to have special singing for the Christmas season as well as the Watch Night service on New Year's Eve. If all went well, they would organize a group to go caroling on Christmas Eve.

There would be new songs to learn for the Easter Services as well. He arranged their seating so that the newer members were interspersed with the older ones. This wise plan would not only give them the support of more experienced voices, but would also discourage any temptation for conversation that would interrupt the orderliness of this important endeavor.

When they were finally dismissed at ten after four, everyone knew the importance of rushing home to do the inevitable chores before they had to hurry back to the evening service. Karl was disappointed he had had no opportunity to say anything to Maria. But his sister encouraged him by reporting all that Maria had said to her.

And so days and weeks went by, until it was just a week before Christmas. The students were unusually restless, and Elder Ziebet was dismayed at his inability to keep order. He knew that this was evidence that a storm of major proportions was brewing, and he saw the clouds gathering in the northern sky even as he called the students in after they had had their lunch recess. By two o'clock the skies had darkened, and the first flakes began to fall. Pastor Epp came in unannounced and suggested the students be dismissed lest calamity should befall them. He cautioned the older students to make sure the younger ones were safe, and asked Hoinz and his friend Isaac Peters to make sure the three younger Ratzloff children got home safely. Tina, Franz, and Ella Ratzloff had no older siblings.

Every house they passed on their way home already had a kerosene lamp in the window and an anxious mother waiting at the door for her children. Hoinz and Isaac left the Ratzloff children safely at their mother's door and then turned to find their own way home. Although they had some difficulty in the strong wind and blowing snow, they both made it safely, to the great relief and thanks of their families.

Snow or blow, the animals had to be fed and bedded down for a long, cold, winter night. Father had already brought them into the barn, and the chickens had gone to roost as soon as the darkness of the storm approached. It was, however, Maria's duty to gather the eggs, while Father, Sarah, the younger Hoinz, and Katie did the milking. Abraham was responsible for the sheep at the other end of the barn. They made their way through blinding wind and snow. What a relief to finally reach the relative warmth and comfort of the barn. Maria finished gathering the eggs and feeding the chickens before the others finished the milking. She sat on a milk stool to wait for them. It would be safer if they returned to the house together. The storm was definitely increasing in strength. Six barn cats sat watching and waiting. They expected their feeding bowl to be filled with rich, foamy, warm milk as soon as the last cow was milked. This would supplement their diet of mice, whose presence in the barn they were expected to keep at a minimum.

Before the children finished milking, they heard the barn door slam against the wall, and snow-covered Father entered. He shook the snow from his coat and fastened the end of a rope to a hook near the door.

"The storm is getting worse, and we'd better make sure the animals have extra feed. We may not get back here very early in the morning."

He made sure everything was done and there was plenty of feed for the animals in case the storm persevered and they would be unable to reach the barn in the morning. Any water they provided would no doubt freeze before morning, but if the animals had access to the small pen on the south side of their shelter, they could survive with snow. When all was done to his satisfaction, they gathered at the door to return to the warmth of the house.

"Cornelius, you go first and try to get your bucket of milk back to the house safely. Sarah and Katie, you follow Hoinz. Be sure you hang on to the rope I brought. It is tied to the kitchen door. Now all of you be sure to hang on to this rope. If you let go, you will surely get lost in this blinding storm. I will be last and bring the eggs with me. Don't loiter. God willing, we will get to the house safely."

They made quite a procession as they stepped out into the darkness of the storm. Father led the way, with the others trying to step into his tracks. A sudden gust of wind hit Maria, and she fell down into a snowdrift, dragging Abraham with her. Father managed to get them upright, and they continued. What a relief it was for Father when at last he bumped into the back door. They tried to shake off the snow from their coats and boots, and then stepped into the warm kitchen. The wind had blown some of the milk out of the buckets, but at least some of it was left. This was taken to the pantry where the cream would rise to the top. Then Mother would skim it, and they would have cream for their coffee and some for making butter. The cream could also be poured over warm bread pudding and other desserts. A dozen eggs were put into the pantry; the rest were taken to the cellar, where they were very carefully put in a large stone jar into a solution of water along with the extras from previous days. With this cold snap, the hens would lay less frequently, but the family would still have plenty of eggs to eat and to use in cooking.

They soon had their outer clothing hung up on hooks behind the stove to dry and gathered around the table for the evening meal.

Mother had made some *Kumst Borscht*[5] with a ham bone. The newly baked rye bread with butter added to a deliciously comforting meal. Tonight the family stayed in the kitchen, huddled near the kitchen stove. The open oven door gave off just enough heat to keep the family warm as they continued to sit around the supper table. Katharina suggested Hoinz get the extra bricks from the front steps and place them in the oven. If they could be heated, they would

---

[5] *Kohlsuppe*, or cabbage soup

provide warmth for those who would soon have to climb the stairs to the unheated bedrooms above.

After the dishes were washed, Father suggested they do a little singing, and all too soon it was time to go to bed. Father read the scripture and asked God's blessing and protection on those who had been caught in the storm.

After the evening prayers, Mother pulled the bricks from the oven and wrapped them in old towels. She handed one to each of the older children. They were happy to know that, when they crawled into bed, the area around their feet would be warm.

The lamps were blown out, and all was quiet except for the howling of the wind.

Maria cuddled up to Margaret, and together their bodies warmed the bed. They soon fell asleep to the mournful music of the howling wind.

Chapter Four

The blizzard lasted three days, after which the sun came out. But the air turned bitterly cold. Father, with the help of Hoinz and Cornelius, scooped a path to the well and to the barn, the paths most used, and the family resumed their normal routine. School reopened, although some of the younger children were kept at home. Fear of illness in the extreme cold convinced mothers that little ones were better off at home. They were kept busy on their letters and numbers by mothers or older sisters.

After a few days the weather warmed, and the little ones were pleased to see their friends and their beloved teacher again. They eagerly took up their reciting where they had left off. They were especially eager to learn their Christmas songs for the program which their parents and grandparents would attend.

Maria, Johann, and Peter were heard singing bits and pieces of "*O, Vienass Boem, O, Vienass Boem, wie grün sind deine Blätter!*"[6] What they lacked in melody was made up in volume. And often Mother would have to hush them, saying, "Enough already."

Then came the eventful day that altered the family plans for weeks to come. Peter Weins rode into the yard one Saturday afternoon. He

---

[6] *O Tannenbaum, O Tannenbaum...* O, Christmas Tree, O Christmas Tree: How very green your leaves!

took his horse directly to the barn where Father was oiling the harnesses. Sarah saw him coming and immediately became very busy cleaning the sitting room. Mother looked out through the kitchen window and commented, "I wonder what Peter wants. I hope no one is sick at the Weins' house. Perhaps he needs Father to help with their horses."

No one replied to her comments, and no reply was expected. Soon Father and Peter came walking to the house, and Father motioned Mother to come into the sitting room. Sarah was about to leave, but Father indicated she should stay. Nervously she sat down on the bench next to the stove, not daring to look up at either of her parents or Peter.

Then Father cleared his throat and said, "Mother, this young man has asked for our daughter's hand in marriage. What do you say to that?"

Nervously, Mother twisted the corner of her apron before she replied, "I don't know ... Sarah is a great help to me, and I hate to see her leave our family. I know she will make a good wife for you, Peter. Will you promise to be a good husband to her?"

Peter stammered, "I will do my best. I have saved quite a few rubles, and Mr. Franz has promised me steady work this next year. I have a cow, and the horse I rode is paid for. I think we will be able to make it." He wiped his brow. This was the most difficult task he had ever encountered.

Father turned to Sarah, "Well, daughter Sarah, what do you say to all this?"

In a voice barely audible, Sarah replied, "I would like to be Peter's wife."

Peter grinned as Father stood and reached his hand out to Peter. "Welcome to the family, Son." Then he turned to Mother. "Let's have some *Faspa*[7]!"

The rest of the family stood in awe as the four came back into the kitchen, and Mother hurried to the stove to get the coffee ready. She took down her special porcelain platter and heaped it with *Tvaebuck*[8]. She even got some of the apple butter from the pantry.

The children were amazed. What had made this ordinary Saturday afternoon into such a special occasion?

They soon found out as Father said the prayer. "And bless the union of these our children to Your honor and glory." After the prayer ended, Father explained to the younger children that Peter Weins would soon join their family by marrying their sister Sarah.

Sarah's siblings stared at the betrothed with gawking eyes, while Peter's and Sarah's faces turned beet red.

The children were then instructed not to mention this to anyone. The banns would not be announced in church for another month, and the engagement must be kept secret until then.

Although nothing was said about the upcoming wedding, things changed dramatically. The very next day Peter came over right after dinner in a small two-wheeled cart with a seat just barely wide enough for two. He helped Sarah up, and the two rode to the singing together while the other children walked through the snow.

Everyone in the community understood what was going on, but nothing would be said about it until the banns had been announced in church.

---

[7] *Abendessen*, an ethnic afternoon lunch on Sundays or special occasions
[8] *Broodjes*, ethnic dinner rolls usually made on Saturdays for Sunday *Faspa*

Meanwhile, preparations continued for the Christmas festival beginning on Friday night, Christmas Eve. The chores were done early. Sarah was in charge of supper. Mother sat near the washstand, which had been moved into the kitchen since the weather had turned cold. The younger children were lined up nearby. Using a washcloth and plenty of soap, she scrubbed each of the children in turn. She scrubbed their necks, ears, elbows, and hands until they were red. Why did those elbows get so dirty? That rough skin looked like pigskin. "Hold still!" she repeated often as she continued to scrub. All the while she was also supervising the foot washing in the washtub nearby. "Now scrub a little harder. Those knees look terrible. There, just look at that heel!" Although the children complained, they knew that this usual Saturday ordeal would not have to be repeated the next day.

After each child was properly scrubbed, all were sent into the parents' bedroom, where clean long underwear had been laid out for each. Katie was there to help the youngest get dressed: first the underwear, then the long stockings, one or two petticoats for the girls, and finally, the very best dress or pants and shirt.

Bibs and aprons were put on the younger ones with warnings not to spill at the supper table. Supper was eaten quickly. Everyone was excited about the Christmas program, so appetites were quickly satisfied. No one had spilled milk on himself or herself, and at last they were all ready to go to the Christmas Eve service. Father had brought the team and wagon to the back door. Hot bricks were brought from the oven and placed in the straw in the wagon box. Father laid a horse hide over the top of the younger ones, while the older ones huddled together in their warm coats and shawls. Mother sat up front on the seat with Father.

When they arrived at the meeting house, several families had already gathered. Many voices were heard calling out, *"Fröhliche Weihnachten[9]."*

The men secured the horses, placing the horse hides on their backs. It was bitterly cold. The women and children hurried into the church.

Everyone was in a festive mood. Mothers were nervous about having their young children recite, but not as nervous as the children themselves. "Now be sure to look at me when you recite, and speak very loudly so everyone can hear," mothers said. More than one mother was heard whispering this in the children's ears: "Stand up straight, and don't fidget."

The evening consisted mostly of singing the old familiar Christmas songs, with the scripture from Luke's gospel being quoted by various children in between. The choir sang beautifully; it was good to have the organ accompanying them this year. Katharina thought of the controversy when plans were made to purchase the organ a year ago. Several in the congregation had been opposed to it, saying it was an unnecessary expense and "worldly." But after they had heard the music, they reluctantly approved and agreed that it really did improve the singing. She looked over at the older people sitting in the front row. Several of them remembered singing, *"O, Du Sehlige, O, Du Fröhliche"[10]* back in Prussia. Old Mrs. Penner was wiping a tear from her eye. No doubt she was thinking about the difficult move from Prussia and now anticipating an even more difficult move to the New World. It brought a lump to Katharina's own throat, but she

---

[9]   Merry Christmas
[10]   *Oh, Thou Holy One; Oh, Thou Joyful One*

swallowed it and determined to sing louder. "Whatever will be, will be." There would be time enough later to worry about that.

After the service, the men hurried out to retrieve their wagons, while the mothers made sure the children were bundled up for the ride home. Fortunately, none had very far to go.

Despite all the excitement, the younger children fell asleep even before they arrived home. The older children helped carry them in while Father and Cornelius unhitched the horses and bedded them down for the night.

In spite of their late bedtime on Christmas Eve, the children were up early the next morning to see what they would find in their dinner plates from Father Christmas. They were not disappointed: They found various sweets, *Paepa Naeta*[11] with raisins, and also several pieces of molasses candy in each plate. "Now you can eat one piece of candy, but you had better save the rest for later today," Mother warned. "Otherwise you will get sick!"

It was hard to resist, but they obeyed, and when afternoon came, they were glad they had.

On the second day of the holiday, the excitement was even greater because Peter Weins and his family would come for dinner. The children would have a great time while the parents would discuss the wedding plans.

After the Christmas and New Year's holiday activities, the Epp family took on a frenzy. Mother and Sarah were busy sewing from early till late. The geese were plucked for a new feather comforter for Sarah. Another hog was butchered so there would be plenty of *Schinken Fleisch*[12] for the wedding feast. The house was cleaned

---

[11] *Pfeffernüsse*, or peppernuts (small spicy cookies)
[12] *Schinken*, or ham

from top to bottom. Special paper was purchased, and Sarah laboriously wrote out the invitation as dictated by her father. The pastor would read this from the pulpit on the fifth of January, and then it would be handed to the first name on the back of the paper, who would deliver it in person to the next name, until all who were invited had received it.

Chapter Five

The day of the wedding arrived. The horses and wagons were lined up at the church. Inside, the crowd hushed as Pastor Epp came in from the side door near the pulpit. The organ began to play, and Sarah and Peter came in from the back of the church. The congregation strained their necks to see their somber faces. The ladies silently *ooh'ed* and *aah'ed* at Sarah's new dress as the couple walked slowly to the front of the church. The choir sang, "Holy, Holy, Holy," and the preacher rose to preach a long sermon about the serious step this couple was taking. He reminded them about the scriptures that sanctified marriage and went on and on about the responsibilities of both the bride and the groom.

Peter and Sarah hardly heard what was said, but they stood solemnly looking at the pastor. From time to time they sneaked a side glance at each other. After it was confirmed that no one in the congregation objected to the union, Pastor Epp came to the part where they vowed to fulfill their duties as husband and wife. "What God hath joined together, let no man put asunder," intoned Pastor Epp. And with a closing prayer, he invoked God to bless the union and all the people present. The ceremony was over.

Mother and Father hurried the family into the wagon for the trip home. They had to be ready to greet the guests who would be arriving for the wedding dinner. Hoinz and Cornelius had been instructed as to where the wagons were to be parked. He was to help the men unhitch the horses and tie them to the back of the wagons, where they would have a portion of oats to eat while the people celebrated with a feast in the house.

Peter and Sarah stood at the entrance to the house to greet the incoming guests. The entire first floor had been set up to feed the crowd. Beds had been taken apart and stored on the second floor. More tables had been constructed of boards on sawhorses. Many of their friends had brought benches of their own and extra ones from the church so everyone would have a place to sit while they ate. Neighbors and friends took over the kitchen, where huge kettles of *Plumamos und Schinken Fleisch* were being kept hot. Friends of the couple served the honored guests, and at last it was time for the kitchen help and the children to eat. There was plenty of food, and with routine dishwashing, everyone had had a plate and a bowl. Burnt sugar cake and peppernuts were served for dessert.

All too soon it was time for the guests to go home. Everyone had chores to do. A few close relatives stayed to help with the cleanup. Their chores would have to wait this once.

The wedding was over. The house again was in proper order. The bride and groom had retired to Sarah's bedroom. Katie would have to double up with Maria and Margaret for this one night. Tomorrow Sarah and Peter would move their gifts and a few pieces of furniture to Peter's parents' place where they would set up housekeeping in what had been the summer kitchen. This small building near the kitchen door was not used in the wintertime and would do until a proper house could be found for the newlyweds.

Life resumed its ordinary routine. At the Epp home, Sarah would often be mentioned. She was missed, but the whole family was happy for her, and they looked forward to the Sundays when she and Peter would come to visit. Maria now slept upstairs with Katie, and Margaret was allowed to move up, too. Both Maria and Margaret felt they had taken a step forward in the growing up process.

The following Sunday Mrs. Nuefeldt came rushing to greet Katharina before the service started. She was very excited. "I have received a letter from Mr. Nuefeldt. They have arrived safely in Nebraska. They had a safe voyage. America is more civilized than he expected. New York City is as big as Petersburg, with buildings that almost reach the sky." She rushed on. "The trains in America are much faster than in Russia. It took them only four days to go from New York City to Lincoln, Nebraska." And then in a lower voice she added, "He says he wishes I had come with him. He is lonesome for my *Tvaebuck* and *Plumamos*."

Mrs. Nuefeldt was so excited, tears came to her eyes, which she quickly wiped away. Katharina hugged her and said, "God be thanked. They had a safe trip." And they walked arm and arm into the church.

Pastor Epp had also received a letter signed by all three men. He reported to the congregation the basics that Mrs. Nuefeldt had reported, but added, "The committee has asked us to pray that they will have wisdom in all the decisions they will need to make. The agent for the Burlington Railroad Company met them in New York. He was very gracious and helped them in every way he could."

He explained what the Burlington Railroad Company was willing to offer: land for as little as three dollars an acre. When the committee had suggested they wanted also to look at some land offers in Kansas and in Canada, he had become even more generous, offering to dig a water well for every section of land purchased. Pastor Epp continued, "The men wish to spend some time in these different areas, so they have asked us to help their families with the spring planting, should their return be later than expected."

Tentative plans were made for immigration if the men should return with a favorable report. The pros and cons of immigration were discussed everywhere. The men talked about it every time two or more happened to meet. The women discussed it as well. The opposing views were held equally. The children debated it at school.

Maria and Abraham were all in favor of migrating. Their friend Karl was also in favor, but he knew his father was totally opposed to it, so he dared not say much. Soon after that, Mrs. Nuefeldt got another letter with glowing reports. Karl was walking home from school with Abraham and Maria, the younger children running ahead.

Karl remarked to no one in particular, but in a way that Maria was sure to hear, "I wish my father wasn't so opposed to the move. If you folks move, we'll likely never see each other again." Then he stepped a little closer to Maria and spoke more softly. "I suppose you will meet some rich American and forget all about me."

Her face flashed red and she didn't look at him but replied so he barely heard what she said. "Maybe your father will change his mind and you will come at a later date."

Karl replied, "If you want me to, I will come by myself when I'm of age."

And again Maria replied in a voice barely audible, "That would be nice."

Sarah came home periodically to visit her family while Peter was busy working. On one occasion the topic of immigration was

mentioned. Sarah said to her mother, "You know, Peter is very interested in going to Nebraska, but he feels a big responsibility toward his
parents. They are growing old and are not very well. I can't imagine
having you and all my family leave without me going with you."

Mother replied in a very somber tone. "You must, of course, be
in submission to your husband." And then wiping a tear from her eye,
she said, "How can I leave you behind? And what will become of
those two grave markers there by the oak tree? I don't know how I
can leave this place. Many of our friends and relatives will no doubt
go, but how I will miss those we leave behind. We must trust God
to work it out. I can understand Peter wanting to stay for his parents'
sake. They are too old to make the trip. God willing, maybe you can
come at a later date."

"Maybe," said Sarah. "But sometimes it is very difficult to wait
for God to work things out."

Scenes like this occurred in many of the households of the little
community. One thing they all agreed on: They were anxious for the
committee to return.

One Sunday morning in late May, Mrs. Fast could hardly contain
herself. She waved a letter to everyone even before she got out of her
wagon. "They have looked at many places, and they want one more
trip to Nebraska. Then they will come home."

There was great rejoicing as the congregation gathered that
morning. Everyone was anxious to hear what the letter said, but there
wasn't much other information. They would just have to wait for the
men to return. Perhaps they could expect them in June.

Meanwhile, crops and gardens had to be planted. The animals
had to be cared for, the laundry had to be done, and myriad other
things had to be tended to. So the time passed quickly. At last the

committee of three arrived back in the little village of Molotschna. The men were exhausted from their travels but scheduled a community meeting two days after their return.

Chapter Six

There was standing room only in the meeting house. Some late-comers found no room and so stood by the open windows, eagerly listening to the reports of the men.

The pastor offered an opening prayer. He prayed earnestly and long, thanking God for the men's safe return. He intoned for wisdom in all that should be said and also wisdom in all decisions that would be made. Ben Franzen later commented that he couldn't understand what made the preacher's prayers so long. Anyone could thank God for blessings and ask for wisdom in just a few words, whereas it always took the preacher at least fifteen minutes. He was chided by Mr. Fast for criticizing the pastor, but several in the congregation agreed with his thought.

At last Mr. Nuefeldt began. "We had a very good trip, thank God. The weather was, for the most part, good. We encountered a major snowstorm in early April while we were in Canada, but God kept us safe. We were with fellow Mennonites who had migrated twenty-five years ago. They were well settled and said they had learned to live with the long winters. The long hours of sunlight in the summer made up for those winter nights, causing their crops to grow more rapidly during the growing season. It was very open country – not many trees. Their houses were warm and comfortable. The area in

South Dakota also had many good qualities, as did the area we visited in what is called Kansas. The committee agreed that the area in Nebraska seemed to be the most desirable. The Burlington Railroad Company representatives were very gracious, offering us many benefits not found in the other areas. They offered us housing in New York while we took care of legal matters there. They have offered us special rates for railroad passage from New York to Nebraska. They have also offered us land for three dollars an acre if we pay cash. If we need financing, they want six dollars an acre, to be paid off in ten years. With a little bargaining, they even offered to dig one well for every section sold.

"They assured us that any kind of equipment for farming or building could be purchased in Lincoln, Nebraska, and delivered to the town of Sutton by the railroad at minimal cost. From there it would be easy enough to haul it by wagon to each homestead. In good faith, we reserved twenty sections of land. The Burlington Railroad Company will hold this land for us for one year. They would like to know as soon as possible whether we want it or not."

As Mr. Nuefeldt paused in his talk, Mr. Unruh spoke up. "What about the barbarians in that country? Are we likely to have the top of our head removed before we get settled?"

Mr. Fast replied, "We did not see any of those so-called barbarians. In fact, the people we met said they hadn't seen any Indians for over two years. The government has moved them to certain areas where they can live, and the army makes sure they stay there."

"How will we build shelters for our families if there are no forested areas nearby?" another spoke up.

"The native grass is short and curly. It grows very tight. Houses have been built by cutting it into blocks and digging it up with a little bit of soil clinging to the roots. This makes a very warm house in the winter which stays cool in the summer. It is free material from the land; it's hard work, but well worth it. We spent one night with the Unruhs north of Sutton. They started with what is called a sod house, but after a year they plastered the inside and put lumber over the outside. It was very comfortable, and it looked nice, inside and out. Glass for windows is easily available in Lincoln."

"How much will all this cost?" Mr. Mireau now asked. "It seems to me that the trip alone will take all the money we have. It isn't cheap to travel by train or ship."

"You are absolutely right," replied Mr. Jantzen. "It will take a lot of money to travel. But if we get a good-sized group, we can get discounts, both from the railroad company and from the steamship company. I firmly believe this is a great opportunity for us Mennonites. All the brethren we spoke to wherever we went were happy they had made the move. America is a strange country, very different from the countries we have lived in. The people determine who is in charge, not some king or czar that claims he has been appointed by God. If the president doesn't do what is right, the people can vote him out of office. Here we simply have to obey and pay exorbitant taxes or else bribe the local governor so he will look the other way." Mr. Jantzen spoke emphatically of what they all knew to be true.

After several hours of more discussion, a relative stranger near the back of the room spoke up. He politely asked the chairman if he could speak to the group for a few minutes. "He must be from Petersburg," several were heard to whisper. "He is not a Mennonite."

"*Guten Tag[13]!* Let me introduce myself. I am Mr. Todtleben, a representative from Czar Alexander. He sends greetings. You remember what a great deal you were given by the Great Czar of Russia when you were being oppressed in the land of Prussia. Here you have developed this fine land into productive farm land. You have maintained your own schools, your own language, your own industry in beer making, and, as if that wasn't enough, the Czar has given you exemption from serving in the military for another ten years. You have reaped benefits at the cost of others who fought to remove the hated Turks from this land. Do you want to risk all this to go to some unknown country where you know not what will become of you?"

"What assurance can you give us that these benefits will continue?" Mr. Mireau asked.

Mr. Todtleben replied, "I have in my hand a paper from the Czar himself extending all these privileges for the next ten years."

Now Mr. Nuefeldt spoke up. "And then what? After the good farm land in America has all been taken, you will continue the oppression?"

After a few more comments, Mr. Todtleben left. He realized he was getting nowhere with this stubborn group of people. They were a tight-knit group and were well known for driving stiff bargains.

Mr. Jantzen took the floor again. "I think we have discussed the issue well enough already. Let me see a show of hands for those who are interested in making the move. You will not be held to this decision. If something comes up that makes it necessary for you to change your mind, your revised decision will be accepted. Vote in good faith."

But Mr. Penner interrupted. "Before we vote, let me say that I and several others here would very much like to make the move. But I must

---

[13] Good day

56

humbly say, I don't have the money for the trip, let alone the funds to buy land in America. What hope is there for me and my family? What kind of financing is there available for those of us that are so poor?"

Mr. Mireau asked for permission to respond to this comment. He said, "God has been very good to my family, and there are others here equally blessed. I would think that those of us that are well off would be willing to help those less fortunate. I move that we set up a general fund to which anyone can contribute with set plans for those who borrow from it to repay in a reasonable way and time."

Pastor Epp now spoke. "Let us take up a collection now to see how successful this plan will be. Just indicate on a paper how much you will be willing to contribute to this fund when the need arises."

This seemed agreeable to all, and to the great surprise of everyone, 11,785 rubles were promised.

After this, over a hundred heads of households signed to indicate they were ready to pursue the plan to immigrate. A committee was appointed to collect the money for the financing and distribute it to those in need with suitable arrangements for repayment.

It was recommended that Mr. Mireau contact the railroad company and the steamship company to obtain the best rates for passage as well as for the shipping of their possessions.

Pastor Epp then instructed the men to go home and discuss the matter with their wives.

On the way out, Hoinz spoke to Mr. Nuefeldt. "Would you please have your wife speak to Katharina? Katharina has indicated that she is much opposed to this move. Maybe Lieska can persuade her that this is not as fool-hardy a plan as she thinks."

Chapter Seven

All the way home Hoinz was wondering how he should break the news to Katharina. He realized that she was very opposed to immigrating to America. "I wish she had been at the meeting," he thought. "She would have a totally different viewpoint, I'm sure. I don't know why these things have to be determined only by the men in our congregation. Many of the women could have valuable input. But that's the way it's always been. I think that puts too much pressure on us men. Doesn't the Apostle Paul say somewhere that God sees no difference between male and female, bond or free? I must look that up sometime."

All too soon he reached his home. The kerosene lamp was by the window. Perhaps everyone had gone to bed. Maybe he wouldn't have to say anything until morning. He took his horse to the barn, but before he could remove the saddle blanket, his sons Hoinz and Cornelius entered the barn.

"Well, Father, how did the meeting go?" they asked, almost in unison.

"It went very well. Is your mother still up?" Father answered. "I think I should discuss it with her before I say anything to you. But what do you think of the idea of moving halfway around the world to start a new life?"

"I am ready to move tomorrow," replied Cornelius.

The younger Hoinz hesitated, until his father turned to him with a questioning look. He stammered a bit and then said hesitatingly, "Well, I don't rightly know. I guess it partly depends on the Ben Franzen family. Do they plan to migrate? I have been thinking of their daughter, Lena. I think she would make a good wife for me in a year or so. What do you think, Father?"

His father clapped him on the back. "Well, well, son. We just married off Sarah, and now you want to leave the nest. Soon our nest will be empty. How about you, Cornelius, my boy? Do you have your eye on a young lady, too? Let me tell you this: if the Czar has his way, you will both be in the army before many years are past. What will the ladies think of that? I think our best option is to move to the new country. Their form of government is so different from what we have ever known, but it has succeeded for a hundred years. It is so far away from other countries that the threat of war is not likely. Franzen did sign the paper for those intending to move. So your little Lena will likely be going."

Hoinz's heart leapt, but he tried not to show his excitement to his father or brother. Quite calmly he commented, "I'm all in favor of the move."

Cornelius indicated that he, too, was in favor. And the father and two grown sons walked together to the house where Mother was waiting.

She saw by the look on their faces what the conversation in the barn had been about, and, throwing her apron over her head, she rushed into the bedroom, closing the door behind her.

Father gave the boys a knowing look and motioned for them to go to bed. They would talk more of this in the morning.

Entering the bedroom, his heart ached as he saw his beloved Katharina with her head in the pillow sobbing. He placed his hand gently on her shoulder and begged her to look at him.

"It is not as bad as you think, Katharina. We are not moving to a wilderness. The committee reported that the land was very well civilized. They have nice houses and prosperous farms. I'd say in some ways they are more advanced in comforts than we are. The committee gave a good report. I wish you could have heard it. I don't see why these meetings always exclude the women. Men have the responsibility to make the decisions, but the wives are to be help-mates. So why shouldn't they also hear the reports?

"Now look at me *mein Liebchen*[14]. Why is it so hard for you to think of moving?"

At last the sobs subsided, and Katharina raised her tear-stained face. "We have worked so hard for what we have here. It just seems hard to leave it all behind. And I often think of the two we buried over by the oak tree. I know they are in heaven with the Savior, but while we live here I feel close to them. And what about my parents and yours? They had such high hopes for this part of Russia. What would they think if they knew we were leaving their graves behind? I think of the trees you planted, the apricot, mulberry, and the lilac bushes. Will I never smell those lilacs again?"

"Now, now, my dear, it is true we will have to leave much behind. But when Mireau returns and tells us how much the passage will cost and how much baggage we can take, you may be surprised at what we can take with us." Hoinz continued, "I think we should invite the Nuefeldts for dinner on Sunday. Then you can ask Elder

---

[14] my little one

Nuefeldt more about what the conditions were like in Nebraska. They may have all kinds of fruit trees there. Maybe even lilac bushes and rose bushes.

"What do you think? Should we invite the Nuefeldts to our house for dinner next Sunday? Then you could hear firsthand how things are in Nebraska." With other comforting words he tried to console his wife, and at last she fell asleep with only an occasional sob escaping into her pillow.

Similar conversations were held in various homes in the neighborhood. In some instances, the wife was more adventuresome than the husband, especially if she had sons of military age, and much urging was done to get the man of the house to sign up with the others.

In the Regier household, Fritz was delighted. "Just think," he said to his wife and children. "All these people will want to sell their land. That will drive the price down and, we can double our farming area for little money. And, Thelma," he said, turning to his wife, "wait till the women have to sell all their fancy dishes, lamps, and furniture. They won't be taking fancy dishes with them, for if they do, they will surely be broken in shipment. I will buy it cheap for you, my dear."

Mrs. Regier replied rather timidly, "I don't want to cheat my friends to get their goods. And if so many leave, who will come to my house to enjoy those fine dishes?"

Mr. Regier turned to Karl. "Wouldn't you like to have that fine horse Mr. Franzen has been riding around? I tell you, we'll be able to get it cheap."

Karl shrugged his shoulders and said, "I'd better go tend to the cattle and get the milking done." He dared not disagree with his father. He only wished that he could migrate also, and especially since the Hoinz Epps would be leaving.

In the morning, the elder Hoinz got up early. He wakened his older sons, Cornelius and Abraham. "Come, come, boys, there is much to be done." Then he called to Katie and Maria. "It is time for you to get up. Mother is not feeling well this morning, so you will need to do what needs to be done in her place."

The younger children were soon awake also. They were all hungry, but Katie was firm. "You have to go wash your faces before you can eat. Now don't make so much noise. Mother has a headache, and you will make it worse with all your shouting. Now go, wash!"

Properly subdued, the four younger ones complied. Margaret offered to help set the table, and by the time the men came in from doing the chores, the breakfast was ready.

Father expressed his appreciation to Maria and Katie. "You have done well. The coffee is hot; the cracklings with potatoes and eggs are cooked just like Mother makes them. I suppose soon some young man will find out what good cooks you are and we will lose another daughter."

Katie blushed and murmured, "Thank you."

But Maria replied, "Not likely!"

The morning scripture was read, the prayer was said, and the family ate in silence. It seemed strange to not have Mother at the breakfast table.

Mother made her appearance shortly after the men had left to work in the field. She looked weary, and Maria suggested she take it easy. "Katie and I can do the work today."

Mother replied, "You have done well, and I appreciate it. I will be fine. It's this talk of moving to America that gives me a headache, but we will make it somehow. Where are Peter and Johann? Father wants to invite the Nuefeldts for dinner next Sunday. I think the boys could take a note over to invite them."

Hearing their mother's voice, the younger children came in to see her. When told of the errand, Anna called out, "Can I go, too? I want to go, too! Can I?"

After persuading her to leave her doll behind, it was agreed the three could go together. They were carefully instructed not to speak to anyone on the way and to be on their best behavior. They should wait quietly for Mrs. Nuefeldt to write a note in reply and then hurry back home.

Johann carried the note very carefully while Peter held his little sister's hand. The errand was completed successfully, and with her reply, Mrs. Nuefeldt handed each of them a sugar cookie. Delighted, they hurried back home.

"Now what do you think we should fix for Sunday dinner?" Mother looked at the two older girls.

"Can I make some *Perieschkje*[15]?" asked Maria.

"I think it is time you learned how to do that. I'd better make the dough, but you can cut up the apples and roll out the dough. I think I'll make a chicken with potatoes. I get tired of V*erenika*[16] all the time. And Katie," Mother continued, "how would you like to try your hand at making *Tvaebuck*?"

By the time Sunday came, everything had been done to perfection. The house was properly cleaned, and the cooking was done.

Mrs. Nuefeldt was very complimentary of the meal. When Mother mentioned that almost all of the cooking had been done by Maria

---

[15] a pastry like *Apfelstrudel,* or cut up apples and sugar baked up in a square of pastry dough
[16] a pasta dough filled with cottage cheese, known also as *Käsetaschen*

and Katie, Mrs. Nuefeldt said, "You girls will make some men good wives." And she gave her sons, Tom and Bill, a teasing look.

The conversation soon moved to the upcoming migration. Mrs. Nuefeldt said to Katharina, "I am greatly influenced by the threat of military service for our two sons, since they are approaching the age for the conscription, but after my husband came back from his exploratory trip I am convinced it would be a wise move. It is not like going into an unknown territory. There are already quite a few Mennonites in the country. I think you have some distant cousins living in the Nebraska area. Aren't you related to the Franzens, who moved five years ago?"

"Yes, Abraham Franzen is my mother's second cousin once removed. Did Mr. Nuefeldt see them?"

"Yes. They have a very comfortable house and a beautiful barn. It has room for six horses and ten cows. They have done very well. They were among the first to settle in the area, so they got the first pick of the farmland."

"But how could they build so well when I hear there is no timber in the area?"

"Oh, they ship lumber in daily to York, Nebraska, and then on to Sutton. It is not much of a job to haul it from Sutton to where the Franzens live." Then, glancing at her husband, she continued, "We will try to get a soddy built as soon as we get there. Maybe a year or two later we will either plaster and put siding on it, or just get the lumber to build a new house. It will depend on how things go."

"I just don't see how we could possibly move this household. Is there a ship big enough for all we would have to take?" The move itself just seemed to overwhelming for Katharina to comprehend.

"What will you pack, and what will you leave behind?" she asked her friend.

"We will know better after we get the report from Mr. Mireau. He is dealing with the railroad and the steamship company for tickets and shipping. If anyone can drive a bargain, he can. We should be hearing from him in another week or two," replied Mrs. Nuefeldt.

Mr. Nuefeldt now spoke to the women. "The application papers for exit visas should be in the mail in another week or so ... if the Czar doesn't take it into his head to deny us exit."

This made Hoinz speak up. "Do you think there is a possibility of that happening?"

"According to what that Mr. Todtleben said, there is that possibility; however, I don't think it likely. The Czar is, in my estimation, eager to get rid of us Mennonites, now that we have made this land productive. And there are many native Russians all too eager to take it over."

After some more animated conversation, the Nuefeldts left. Katharina and her daughters cleaned up the kitchen and were soon busy washing the many dishes from the special dinner.

"Mrs. Nuefeldt surely paints a good picture of the Nebraska area. She almost makes me want to move there myself," said Katharina.

Katie answered, "It does seem like an impossible task. The Nuefeldts are a family of only eight, whereas we are a family of twelve, even if we don't count Sarah. That does make a difference, but at the same time, Cornelius, Abraham, Maria, and I are able to help with the packing and so on. I think with God's help, we could make it. I just wish Sarah and Peter were going."

"That is the problem: Too many families will be split apart, and we might never see each other again. I don't think you girls realize how far it is to Nebraska in America."

Chapter Eight

Those who were planning to move to America were anxiously waiting for the paperwork to come from Petersburg. Now that the decision had been made, they were eager to get going. They were also waiting to hear what kind of a bargain Mr. Mireau had made with the railroad company and the steamship company.

The paperwork from Petersburg came first. The townspeople were surprised to see Mr. Todtleben deliver it himself. He brought a German-speaking Russian with him to make sure the Mennonites understood all that was expected of them in filling out the necessary papers. The shocking part was that the government would buy back the land they wanted to sell at the price they had paid for it originally. In spite of all the protesting, Mr. Todtleben would not waiver from this order. This was a tremendous disappointment to those who had worked so hard to improve the condition of the land. What had been useless swamp land was now choice agricultural land since these industrious farmers had laid drainage tile to drain the swamp. All their back-breaking digging and refilling the trenches would now benefit the government. At last Mr. Todtleben agreed to pay them for the buildings and improvements such as wells and windmills on the property. He also agreed to give them a stipend for the crops that had not yet been harvested. With a little monetary consideration, he would expedite the paperwork in Petersburg so they would be able to start to America by the end of July.

It was a disappointed crowd that gathered for the Sunday service. However, Pastor Epp preached a powerful sermon on trusting God for all their needs rather than putting faith in earthly governments. This resulted in even greater determination to leave Russia.

Soon after, Mr. Mireau returned with good news. The railroad company had offered to run a special train for the immigrants if they had at least two hundred passengers, not counting children under five. The little ones under five would travel free, but they would not have reserved seats. Each paying passenger would be given a space equal to an area five feet by five feet for the things they would be taking with them. Their cargo could be stacked six feet high if necessary, as long as it did not exceed the 25-square-foot allotment. This cargo space would not be accessible during the trip, since it would be in freight cars added to the passenger train. The passengers would have the space under their seats and on a shelf above the seats for such items that they would need *en route*. The steamship company was also very considerate. They already had several hundred reservations, and if the Mennonites bought two hundred tickets, *The Teutonia* would be at capacity. The passengers would be given an equal amount of space in the hold for their possessions. However, the steamship's staterooms were larger than the allotted cargo space in the train. So the travelers would have access to more of their belongings while traveling by steamship. Now the preparations began in earnest.

What a challenge it was! Hoinz and Katharina talked long about what to take and what to leave behind. Finally, Hoinz said to his wife, "You have your chest that your grandparents brought from Prussia.

Whatever you can fit into it, you can take. Meanwhile, I will fill the wagon box with what I need. We have an advantage, since Hoinz, Cornelius, Maria, Katie, and Abraham will also be allotted space. Anna, Peter, Johann, and William will have to sit on laps, but I don't think that will be a problem. There may be room on the seat between the older children. I think perhaps we should offer some of our baggage space to those who have smaller families and thus are allotted less space." This was agreeable to Katharina. She was delighted with the amount of space they were given. It was much more than she had expected.

They set about planning. They would take as much food as possible so that they would not have to buy food at any of the train stops. The apricot crop had already been harvested and dried. The early plums were now in the process of drying. Father decided to butcher a hog, even though this was never done until winter time. They could dry some of the meat; other parts could be cured. Some fully-cooked meat could be covered with lard in several stone jars, and that would keep for a long time. Mother and the girls baked extra *Tvaebuck* each time. They separated the two halves and toasted what wasn't eaten on Sundays. These dry buns would not mold and would be a staple on the trip. Dry beans were saved by the bushel. Neighbors who were not going offered their stores of dried raisins and plums in exchange for the crops the migrants were leaving behind.

Farm implements were sold, as was most of the furniture. They had been told that these items could easily be replaced in the new country. Father insisted on keeping the *Klietaschope*[17], since it had been made by his grandfather in Prussia. He gazed in pride at the

---

[17] *Kleiderschrank*, or wardrobe

carved letters HJE attached near the top. The children stood in amazement as he took his screwdriver and unfastened a few screws. In no time at all, the wardrobe was just a stack of neatly packaged lumber; even the two drawers at the bottom came apart to stack flat.

The younger children did not have many toys, but they definitely wanted to take the ones they had with them. Anna insisted on taking her doll. She was persuaded to give the little cradle to her friend Rachel after Father promised to make her another one when they arrived in Nebraska. Peter and Johann each had a stick horse that they insisted on taking. They were told they could take them, but they would have to be responsible for them. If they were lost or left at some place, they could not expect anyone to go back for them.

Mother, with the help of Katie and Maria, went through all the family's clothing. Those items that were worn thin would have to be left behind. If they could be patched or lengthened, it was done. Those items that had been outgrown were packed carefully. They would fit the next child in a few months. Dishtowels and bed linens were inspected for tears or worn spots that could be mended. Mother and her girls looked wistfully at the porcelain tea set that had been Grandmother Franzen's. How could they leave it behind? And yet how could they pack it so it would not be broken? And what about that fancy painted glass kerosene lamp that stood on the little table in the living room? They all burst into tears when Father and Hoinz came in each carrying a wooden box with a close fitting lid. Abraham followed with a bag full of newly sheared wool.

"Maybe, if you pack a lot of this soft wool around the tea set, it will fit in this box. The lamp should fit in the other box. If we pack it carefully, it might make the trip. Put the boxes in between the feather ticks in the chest," Abraham suggested.

There were wool blankets and feather ticks to be folded and packed tightly. Winters in Nebraska were every bit as cold as Russia. It was hard to pack winter coats and shawls on such a warm day, but they would be needed, perhaps even before they reached America.

As the packing was done, the items were stored in the living room. The chest was taken apart and put back together in the barn. It was too wide to go through the doors of the house.

Meanwhile, in the Fast household, Johann came into the house and spoke to his wife, Elizabeth. "Everything is packed and ready to go. The last crate has been nailed shut. Do you have all the household items packed?"

"Yes. The children were so good today that I got the work done without delay. The baby is sleeping, so I will have your supper ready in just a few minutes. You look tired. Why don't you lie down and rest while I finish supper?" Then she turned to her eldest. "Come, Martha, set the table. Albert, you can help Peter and Matilda wash their hands and faces. Now do it quietly; your father is very tired. Let him sleep a little, yet before supper."

Chattering softly, the children went about their tasks. "Tomorrow we will go to church, and the next day we will go on a very long trip," Albert explained to his younger siblings. "We will go in the wagon to a place where they have trains, and we will get on the train and go many days until we get to the ocean."

"What is a train? And what is the ocean?" Peter was curious. Although the children realized that strange things had been going on the last few weeks, they did not understand what was about to happen.

Albert tried to explain. "The train is like many wagons all hooked together. It is pulled by an engine, which is very big and very loud.

The ocean is just a lot of water. Water as far as you can see. Now hold still while I wipe your face."

As Peter resisted and squealed at the cold washcloth, his mother came over.

With her finger to her lips, she whispered, "Hush! Papa is sleeping." The children soon took their places at the table, and Elizabeth tiptoed to the bedroom to check on her husband.

He opened his eyes as she entered the bedroom. "If you can manage the children, I think I will stay here a little longer. You can save me a little of the soup. I will eat it later."

The children were surprised when their mother bowed her head and spoke the prayer. This was something that their father always did. Following the prayer, they ate in subdued silence. It was so unusual for Father to be sick.

Martha and Albert helped with the dishes and then got Peter and Matilda ready for bed while their mother nursed little Mary. Rocking the baby, Elizabeth prayed that all would go well and nothing would delay their plans to travel. Surely Johann would feel better in the morning. It would be a special church service with many farewells to be said.

However, when morning came, Johann was not feeling better. He suggested Elizabeth take the baby and the older children to church. He would be fine, and Peter and Matilda could stay with him. They could play quietly in the bedroom.

"No, my husband, if you don't feel like going, we will all stay home." At her insistence Johann agreed. He was too tired to argue, and he dropped back to sleep.

A little later, when Elizabeth stepped into the bedroom, Johann motioned for her to sit down in the rocker where she usually sat while nursing the baby. "Elizabeth, my dear, no matter what happens I want you on your way tomorrow. We have planned long and hard for this, and I don't want to change anything." He paused, and Elizabeth thought he had dropped off to sleep, but as she rose to return to the kitchen he again opened his eyes. Very softly he continued, "We should have made the trip last year when your family left, but with you being with child, I thought the trip would be too hard. Now you must go, even if you have to go without me. The Epps and Franzens and the other people in the group will help you. God will be with you."

All of Elizabeth's arguments only made Johann more emphatic, and at last Elizabeth realized she was only adding to Johann's discomfort. She finally took his hand and said, "Maybe you will feel better in the morning." And her beloved husband turned his head and went back to sleep.

At the Hoinz Epp house, the family was gathered at the supper table. The conversation centered on what had been packed. Mother commented that she was so glad that she had found room for her washboard, her big soup kettle, and the big baking pans, as well as the large dishpan that doubled as a mixing bowl for her bread and *Tvaebuck* dough. Hopefully, at some place where they would have delays, she would have access to a cook stove so she could replenish her supply of *Tvaebuck*. Everything other than the items needed daily were stacked in the living room. The individual bundles would be wrapped in the bedcovers on Monday before they left. The blankets were needed for tonight and tomorrow night. Yet they would be available for use during the train ride and also the voyage. The final laundry was done. If only the exit visas would come. The family was ready to leave.

Sunday came and the church was crowded. This would be their last service. Many a song was interspersed with sobs as people realized this parting would be permanent. After the service, the congregation gathered under the trees near the church, where tables had been set up for one last common meal. Then goodbyes were said, again with many hugs and tears.

Many in the congregation had noticed that the Fast family was absent. Pastor Epp noticed and made a note to be sure to call on them in the afternoon. He hoped, as did the congregation, that no one was sick. It would be difficult to delay the departure. After he had said the prayer for the meal, he walked over to his brother, Hoinz, and said, "I feel I must go to see what has happened to the Fast family. They never miss church. I hope no one is sick. My wife and I will pay them a visit right away."

Elizabeth Fast was expecting the pastor and his wife. She knew he would come when he realized they were not in attendance. She greeted him warmly and explained what was happening. Mrs. Epp hugged Elizabeth warmly and the three tiptoed into the bedroom. After a few minutes sitting by the bedside, Elizabeth got up to go to the kitchen. "You have not eaten, have you? I have a little soup left from last night. We will share, and I will make some coffee." Mrs. Epp followed her to the kitchen, where Elizabeth could no longer control herself. With tears suddenly flowing freely, she confided in her friend. "He does not think he will get better, and he wants me to go without him. But how can I leave him behind?"

Mrs. Epp put her arms around her friend to console her. "Here. You sit down. I will make the coffee. And where is that kettle of soup? I will heat it up for us."

With the children's help, the table was soon set, the soup was hot, and all but Johann sat down to eat. Pastor Epp prayed earnestly for all at the table and for Johann especially.

Later, as the children went out to play, the three sat at the table talking. Pastor Epp began. "Johann told me of his desire for you, Mrs. Fast, to continue your plans to leave. He wishes to stay behind. His sister and brother-in-law can take care of him. If he gets better, he will join you in America later. Surely there will be other ships going."

With uncontrollable sobs, Elizabeth spoke. "Yes, that is what he told me this morning. But how can I go without him?"

"I know that will be very difficult. We will look after your husband. It is his will that you leave. Maybe he will feel better in the morning. We will leave it in God's hands."

Meanwhile, back at the church, Abraham singled out his friend Karl to wish him farewell. Karl was overcome with grief and disappointment that he was not a part of the group leaving. He vowed that he would come to America just as soon as he was of age. Karl looked around the crowd, and when he saw Maria putting something into the family wagon, he sauntered over. "Maria, I have something for you." And he handed her a little wooden hand-carved robin. "This should help you remember me."

Blushing, Maria replied, "But how will you remember me? I have nothing to give you."

"Aw, shucks, why don't you give me one of those little curls that keep coming out from under your bonnet?" And he took out his prized pocket knife and reached for Maria's hair.

"Oh, don't cut that! Here. Take this," and she shifted her bonnet so he could cut a lock from her neck area where it would not be noticed.

Out of sight of the crowd, Karl suddenly placed both hands on Maria's face and kissed her on the cheek. Maria noticed a tear in his eye as he quickly dashed away back to where the crowd was gathered. She touched the place where he had kissed her, blinked away the tears in her own eyes and rejoined her family.

The crowd gathered to sing "God Be with You till We Meet Again," and the families got into their own wagons. Would they ever see each other again?

At the Fast home, the meager lunch had been eaten. Pastor and Mrs. Epp were getting ready to go back to the church. Elizabeth had just finished nursing the baby. She lay the baby down in the little cradle Johann had made when their first child had been expected. What a good job he had done! The wood had been sanded to exquisite smoothness and then shellacked to a fine shine. She had lovingly stitched the quilt as well as the padding for it. She had even embroidered little flowers on the little pillow. She touched the tiny stitches. This had served for all five of their babies and would no doubt do for others that would come along. The cradle would be left behind, but the little bedding would be wrapped up in the blanket and carried with them, along with blankets for each of the children.

She straightened up to return to her guests in the kitchen. She noticed that Johann was awake and seemed to want to say something. She leaned over to hear what he might have to say.

"Bring the children in. I would like to see them for a minute," he whispered in a voice barely audible.

With that, Elizabeth tiptoed back to the kitchen and motioned for the older four to come into the bedroom. Quietly she led them to her husband's bedside.

Johann reached both hands out to the children, smiled, and whispered, "Help Mama." He paused to catch his breath, and then, with some difficulty, continued. "I know you will be good." With greater difficulty, he asked, "Can you say Psalm 23 for Papa?"

Very solemnly they repeated the Psalm for their papa, with Martha and Albert leading. Matilda and Peter barely knew the words, but they tried to follow their older siblings. Papa squeezed their hands and then turned again to Elizabeth, while she motioned for the children to return to the kitchen. Elizabeth leaned over the bed to catch whatever her husband might say.

"Go with God," he whispered in a voice barely audible, and then he was gone. With a scream heard all through the house, Elizabeth threw herself over him and screamed, "No! No! Don't leave me!!"

The children came running. "Mama, Mama! What is the matter?" And the poor woman had to explain to her little ones that their papa had gone to be with Jesus.

Although the pastor and his wife had been ready to leave, they now took off their wraps. They would stay as long as needed. Mrs. Epp took Elizabeth in her arms and let her sob on her shoulder, while Pastor Epp tried to comfort the children.

At last he left to inform the congregation of the tragedy that had just occurred. After a long time of sobbing uncontrollably with the children clinging to her skirts, Elizabeth raised her eyes to those of her dear friend. Resolutely she broke away from the arms of her friend, walked to the wash basin where she splashed cold water on her face. Then she calmly walked to her precious rocking chair, and, motioning for her children to come sit on her lap, she again told them that their papa had left them to go to be with Jesus.

Little Matilda said, "When will Papa come back?" Elizabeth had to explain that Papa could not come back. She went on to tell them that they would go to America just as they had planned. In America, Grandma and Grandpa would take care of them. They would get to see Uncle Jake and Aunt Grace. Martha and Albert remembered their grandparents and this aunt and uncle, and were comforted by her words. But Peter barely remembered, and Matilda was too young to remember.

With tears still on his little face, Peter said, "I want to go see Grandma and Grandpa, but I want Papa to go with us."

After a few more minutes, Pastor Epp returned with some of the elders. They prepared Johann's body for burial, and then moved it to the church, assuring Elizabeth that a proper burial would be provided, even without the family there.

Mrs. Epp insisted that Elizabeth and the children come to spend the night at her house, which they were more than willing to do.

Just as the first wagon started to leave the church grounds, Pastor Epp drove up. He motioned for the congregation to gather and made the sad announcement of Mr. Fast's death. The congregation was stunned. What now?

Pastor Epp explained the situation and intoned the congregation to support Elizabeth and the children, since they would still be leaving the next day.

It was a somber crowd that left to spend one last night in Russia. What would the future bring?

The Epp family realized that this was the last night they would spend in the home they had learned to love. It was difficult to get to sleep for all but the three youngest. The family was grieved with the news of the death of their friend Johann Fast. They resolved to do all in their power to help the poor widow with her family. It was good that her parents and siblings were in America, where they would take care of this poor widow with five children.

Morning came quickly, and the family was awake early. The children were dressed in their Sunday best, and then their next-to-best was put on over that. "Why do I have to wear two dresses plus my pinafore?" complained Anna. "I'm hot!" The boys complained as well, but Mother explained this was the only way they could take enough clothing with them. She and the rest of the family were also wearing extra clothing. Each person in the family had a bundle tied in a blanket. Each was to be responsible for that bundle at all times. Mother and the older girls each had a basket filled with roasted *Tvaebuck*, dried meat, and some dried fruit in tin boxes. Hopefully, this would be enough food for the family until they reached the port city of Hamburg in Germany. They could buy coffee on the way, but it would be too expensive to buy food for the whole family. They would make do with what they had. Mother packed a tin cup with her things. Her family would not drink out of the common cup that she knew hung by the water pail in the train car.

The exit visas had arrived just two days before. Apparently, Mr. Todtleben had arranged for them to arrive just before the departure date as a means of making the departing travelers more anxious. Mr. Nuefeldt would keep them all together. It would alleviate the necessity for each person to deal with the border agents.

Chapter Nine

It was quite a group that met in front of the church on Monday morning. The wagons were piled high with precious belongings that could not be left behind.

Villagers who were not leaving had been hired to drive the wagons to Hachstadt, where the travelers' possessions would be loaded onto the train. They would then return with the horses and wagons that they had purchased at a very low price. Some of the wagons would have the wheels and running gear removed and be taken on the long trip.

More goodbyes were tearfully said, and at last the wagons began the long trek to the railroad station at Hachstadt. The Hoinz Epp family took the lead. Behind them came Mrs. Fast. Hoinz Epp had suggested that his son Hoinz should drive the wagon for Mrs. Fast, which he was more than happy to do, since she had a good-looking team of spirited horses. Mrs. Fast was dressed in black with her face veiled; only the occasional trembling of her body indicated her intense sorrow. Hoinz reached his hand to help her up into the wagon seat. His father then handed up the baby and helped the other children into their designated places. Martha and Albert were given instructions to take good care of Peter and Matilda in the back of the wagon, where a small space had been left for them to sit on a chest. With a blanket spread over the chest, it would make a fairly comfortable space for them, even if they should fall asleep. Mrs. Fast turned around frequently to make sure they were riding safely. They had been instructed to remain seated at all times, lest they lose their balance and fall off if the wagon should hit a rut.

In all, there were twenty wagons finally on their way to what the *émigrés* hoped would prove to be the promised land for them.

It was a long, wearisome journey to the railroad station. The younger Hoinz's heart ached for the poor widow sitting beside him, but he didn't know what to say to her, so he remained quiet. After some time, he heard the children talking behind them.

Peter was evidently crying. Albert spoke to him consolingly, "Don't cry, Peter; I will take good care of you."

To which Peter replied, "Yes, but I want my papa. When he comes back, he won't know where we are."

Poor Albert had to explain to the little boy that Papa was not coming back.

Then little Matilda woke from a nap and whimpered, "I want to go home now. Papa is waiting for me."

Martha replied, "Papa went to be with Jesus, and we have to go to America to live with Grandma and Grandpa."

As Matilda continued to whimper, Mrs. Fast told Martha to give her a roasted *Tvaebuck*, hoping that would console her. Then the baby began to fuss, and poor Elizabeth was at a loss as to what to do.

Hoinz ventured, "Maybe the baby is hungry. Go ahead and nurse her. I will look the other way."

And so the hours slowly passed until noon, when Mrs. Fast rummaged in the bundle at her feet for food for the family. She offered some dried apricots along with the *Tvaebuck* to Hoinz, which he took thankfully. Soon the children dozed off again. Mrs. Fast also nodded her head a couple of times, and Hoinz finally said to her, "Here. Let me hold the baby. You can maybe get a little sleep. This has been a difficult time for you."

With a sob, Elizabeth agreed and then spoke. "I did not want to leave without my Johann, but I had no choice. We had sold our property in order to buy the passage. Hopefully, we will reach my parents in Nebraska, and they will help me. It is a hard life, but God is faithful. He will not desert us."

Awkwardly, Hoinz took the baby, but when little Mary smiled at him, he was smitten. He was delighted to hold her, and Elizabeth held Peter and Matilda alternately. Hoinz let his mind wander and, in the lazy motion of the wagon, he almost dozed off himself. He could imagine himself riding down the road with Lena beside him. He would not have to turn the other way while she nursed their child. He wondered what that would be like. Hopefully it would come about within a year or two. It was a pleasant daydream.

Later in the day the children again grew restless. Hoinz heard Albert complain, "Mother, Martha is taking up too much room. I can't even stretch my legs, and Peter is just sitting here crying all the time. I wish he would stop. My father is gone too, and I miss him, but I don't cry about it, 'cause crying doesn't help."

Martha retorted rather quickly, "Well, with Mary on my lap, I have to stretch out my legs. I am tired. I wish we could go home. I wish Father was with us. Why did he have to die? I don't think I want to go to America after all."

Poor Mrs. Fast. What could she do? She looked at Hoinz with desperation.

"Whoa," Hoinz spoke to the horses, and they stopped their plodding. He turned to look at the children crowded into a small space in the back of the wagon. "I see you are mighty crowded back there." Then he handed the reins to Elizabeth and got down from his seat. Walking toward the back of the wagon he lifted Matilda, and then Peter, down. Then he helped Martha and Albert get down as well.

"We'll let your mother drive the horses for a little. We'll walk. We'll see if we can keep up with them." The horses were so used to following the wagon ahead of them they needed very little guidance from Elizabeth. Even with the baby back in her lap, all she had to do was call out, "Giddap!" and they continued their steady plod, plod, plod.

After a short time, Hoinz asked if Peter would like to drive the horses for awhile. Peter was thrilled, and Hoinz promised the other three would get their turns as well. They got back into their places with Peter now on Hoinz's lap, reins in hand. When Albert's turn came, Hoinz and Elizabeth made room for him to sit between them. Elizabeth gave Hoinz such a look of appreciation that he blushed and commented feebly, "I remember being a child myself. This has to be hard for them."

Several of the other wagons also stopped periodically while passengers rearranged themselves. Often older children would get down and walk beside the wagon for a time. Occasionally, even the parents would walk for a short distance. They would be happy when they reached Hachstadt. Some of the weary ones were even having momentary doubts about their decision to travel. This would be a long, long journey!

"This is not like riding on top of a load of hay. I never realized what a comfortable ride that was," Maria commented, but no one replied.

When the dust of the wagons ahead became too bothersome, mothers provided wet rags to tie over the faces of those coughing uncontrollably.

The sun was going down when they at last reached Hachstadt. The train was waiting, and the men were soon busy unloading the wagons and loading the freight cars of the train. The women were busy tending to the children and preparing an impromptu meal for their families. The Epps and the Franzens, as well as others, invited Elizabeth and her children to eat with them. Elizabeth appreciated the offer, and her children ate what was offered them. Katharina urged Elizabeth to eat something, and, after a cup of coffee, Elizabeth managed to eat a few dried plums and a roasted *Tvaebuck*.

"You must keep up your strength so you can care for the children, and you must have milk for little Mary," she said.

Hoinz tried to find a place near Lena to eat the evening meal, but she seemed to ignore him. When he finally caught up with her when the meal was over, she spoke. "Did you enjoy riding with the young widow?"

Aha, he thought, *she is offended. Is she jealous?* He assured her that it had been only because of his father's instruction that he had driven the Fast wagon. "I was actually pretending it was you sitting beside me. The way it will be in a few years, I hope." At this her friendly smile returned, and all seemed to be well again.

The children were awed at the sight of the train cars and eager to board, but the parents urged them to run around and get some exercise before they would be confined again.

Soon the engine came roaring down the track, and the younger children dashed to their mother's skirts. Never having seen an engine, they were terrified by the noise and the sight of this huge monster machine coming toward them.

The last of the possessions had been loaded, and the engine backed up to connect to the cars. The conductor motioned for the passengers to board.

With great apprehension, the mothers urged their children to clamor up the steps and find a seat. The older children were eager to inspect the inside of the car, where they would spend the next few days.

The younger Hoinz helped Mrs. Fast with her luggage while Katie helped her with the children. Maria, Abe, and Margaret clamored up after them with Johann and Anna. Father took the baby while Mother managed some of the extra bundles. At last they were settled into their places.

Margaret looked around at the rows of benches and commented, "This looks almost like our church, with the two rows of benches. But it is not as wide."

To which Anna replied, "There is no place for the preacher."

"I hope we won't have to listen to some ol' preacher talk the whole time," Abraham commented. Although several other teenagers agreed, they dared not speak about it.

"I just hope this will be a little more comfortable than riding in that crowded wagon," Margaret said as she settled in her seat with her bundle at her feet.

"It is a sure thing we cannot get out and walk for a change," replied Dietrich Franzen, to which they all gave a chuckle.

When the family members were all accounted for, the conductor called, "All aboard!" and in another few minutes they heard the *chug, chug*, as the engine began the task of pulling the heavy load. As the engine began its slow process of getting each car moving, the passengers were surprised, and some almost lost their balance as their car experienced that first tug. But after the train was at full speed, they learned to sway with the motion, and soon several were rocked to sleep.

Katharina and Hoinz wondered how they would endure sitting on the hard wooden benches for six days, as did many of the other passengers, especially the older ones. Elizabeth and her five children had the last two seats in the same car with the Epps and the Franzens. She thanked Hoinz for driving her to the station and offered him the seat that had been designated for her husband, but Hoinz declined, choosing rather to sit with his friends so she would have more room for her younger children who were sitting on the laps of the older two.

They all marveled at the accommodations in the train car. At one end of the car there was a wooden barrel filled with water for drinking. A dipper hung on a nail nearby. Across from this was a separate little room with a door barely big enough for the adults to pass through. Inside was a bench with round holes cut out. Looking through the holes they could see the ground passing by under them. Fathers explained what this was for, and some of the younger ones were eager to try it. Mothers warned the younger children to be careful when using this facility, to prevent their falling through.

There were several other families in the car as well as a few single men and women who had left parents behind to seek a future in the new world. Introductions were made, as some had come from neighboring villages and had not met before. They enjoyed lively conversation for some time, but as darkness fell, everyone began to arrange blankets to provide a sleeping environment for children and adults alike. Soon soft, deep breathing and some snoring was all that could be heard. Occasionally a baby cried to be fed, or young children whimpered, but all in all, the night passed without incident.

When morning came, the conductor walked through the train announcing that in a half hour they would reach the town of Losawaja. The train would stop there for one hour to load coal and water for the engine. The passengers were welcome to disembark, and they could find food and coffee to buy in the station house.

The adults anticipated hot coffee with eagerness, and although the children had done some walking up and down the aisles, they too wanted to get out. Anxious mothers counted heads and instructed older children to watch the little ones. "Hold on to their hands so they don't get lost or left behind," the mothers admonished the older ones.

Legs felt wobbly as they stepped on solid ground after having to keep their balance on the swaying of the train cars. But it was a welcome relief to stretch and walk around.

Abraham and Maria decided to look around the area, being careful to stay near the train depot. They could see that this town was much bigger than Hachstadt. Tempted to walk up the street, they spoke to the conductor, who told them the train would not wait for them, but that they had enough time to go for a short distance. Along the street, Maria picked a few flowers that were different from any she had ever seen. Soon they heard the whistle of the engine and hurried back to the depot. Just in time, they clamored aboard, to the consternation of their parents who scolded them properly. Mother was pleased with the flowers but suggested Maria give them to Mrs. Fast at the end of the car. As she walked down the narrow aisle, the train gave a sudden lurch, and she fell headlong. Greatly embarrassed, she scrambled to her feet. Passengers nearby aided her, and she was not hurt, except for a bruised ego. Mrs. Fast accepted the flowers, but instead of thanking her, a tear trickled down her cheek. Maria patted Mrs. Fast on the shoulder and returned to her own seat. No thanks were necessary. This time Maria was careful to hang onto the backs of the seats to prevent herself from falling, and she arrived at her own seat safely.

Through the afternoon, different age groups gathered in different parts of the train car. As the younger children became restless, Luella Ott gathered the younger children together and began telling them Bible stories. With her two brothers, Franz and Isaac, from the village of Klippenfeld, Luella was hoping to find a new life in America. Their parents had both died from the disease recently. Luella told the fascinating Bible story of how Abraham had traveled to a foreign country at God's direction. He didn't even know where he would end up. She continued, "We know where we hope to end up, and we believe God will help us just as He helped Abraham." Then she asked the children what they expected to experience in Nebraska.

The replies were varied. Martha Fast spoke up first. "I will see Grandma and Grandpa and Uncle Jake and Aunt Margaret. Grandma will have *Zucker Kuka* [18] for us. And Uncle Jake will play with us. He always makes us laugh."

Albert agreed with her and said, "Maybe Grandpa will make another stick horse for me. My old one is broken. Maybe I will get a real horse, and he will make the stick horse for my little brother Peter."

John Franzen spoke next. He expected to see big buildings and big ships, bigger even than the buildings of Hachstadt. His brother expected to see big wild wolves and maybe buffalo. And then he mentioned wild Indians. This served to frighten the other children, so Luella comforted them by telling them that Mr. Nuefeldt had not

---

[18] or *zucker keks:* sugar cookies (also known as *Plätzchen*)

seen any Indians, and she had heard that there were some, but they were friendly.

The older group of children had gathered in another area of the car and were discussing their own expectations. Most of them expected to be farmers like their fathers. The girls hoped to have comfortable homes, with flowers around the front yard. Most of them expected to have schools where they could further their education.

Abraham Epp hoped to learn to speak English and learn to communicate with other people. Maybe he would get a job with the railroad company and drive a train all over the new country. Maria had her heart set on being a school teacher, while John Franzen planned to get educated to be a doctor. Several indicated that they did not like all the hard work of farming, and planned to be merchants in the towns that would surely develop in the new country.

The mothers discussed their children, their sewing, and other fancywork. Several had brought knitting and crochet work with them and were busy working at it as they visited. They spoke with sadness of the deceased members of their families they had left behind. They were hopeful for the future but did not have high hopes for an easy life.

The men discussed farming opportunities in the new country, where they would have less interference from the government. Several had not owned land in Russia, and their hopes were high to own land in the new country.

"With the wheat seed we have with us, we will harvest great crops. Mr. Jantzen said that the black topsoil was a foot deep. I can't wait to see that wheat grow," said one of the rising farmers. He reported that there were always new methods of farming being developed, and he was eager to try some of them himself. He had seen a reaper invented by a man named McCormick that could cut ten times as much as a good man could cut with a scythe. The machine not only cut the wheat, but it also automatically tied it into uniform bundles. The machine was pulled by horses. The farmer sat behind in comfort while the horses did the work.

Some of the older men scoffed at this. "Doesn't the Good Book say that with the sweat of his brow a man shall eat his bread?"

And so the day ended and the scheduled stop for coal and water for the engine was again announced.

The travelers knew they had more days to bounce around on those hard wooden benches. Occasionally they would get up and walk up and down the narrow aisle just to get some exercise. The children soon learned to run up and down the aisle without losing their balance. And many a parent had to stop their activity as the commotion disturbed fellow passengers.

And so the days went by one after another. On the third day, Anna Franzen complained of a sore throat, and everyone was anxious about an outbreak of disease that would interfere with their plans. Even though her mother could tell she had a fever, there wasn't much she could do about it. The other children were told to stay away from her, and after she had had a long nap she indicated she felt much better. Thanks were given to the Lord for this, and supplication was made for health and strength for the continuing journey.

Those who had looked forward to days of inactivity after their summer of strenuous labor tired of the inactivity of the trip plus the constant swaying of the cars and sudden lurches as the train either came to a stop at a village or as it started out again. They longed for even the labor of walking behind the plow. Six days of total inactivity became very tiresome.

Everyone was excited as they reached the border of Germany. Now it would only be two more days of train travel. They could feel they were really on their way, now that they were finally leaving Russia. There was some delay as travel passports were inspected individually. But eventually all the papers had been stamped, and they boarded a new train. The engineer and trainmen as well now spoke German rather than Russian. Although it was the High German, most of the immigrants could understand at least some of it. After all, it was the language of the Bible and their church services. Abraham tried to speak to the trainmen. The engineer tried to explain how the engine worked. Abraham was fascinated and tried to explain the workings to the other people around him.

The weary passengers were pleased that this train seemed to go much faster, and slowed and restarted much more smoothly than the Russian trains had done. They eagerly looked out the windows when the conductor announced they were going through the villages where their ancestors had lived almost a hundred years before. The farms where grandfathers and great grandfathers had worked so hard were still productive. As the train crossed the Vistula River, the older people strained to see the land their ancestors had drained so that it could become profitable farm land.

As they neared the end of their travel by train, the travelers were filled with both anticipation and apprehension. Had this really been a wise move? *What if...?* And anxieties filled the hearts of even the most enthusiastic travelers. The decision had been made: They could not return. They resolutely set their faces to the future. The children, sensing their parents' anxieties, became fretful as fears filled their minds as well.

Chapter Ten

The conductor entered the car and called, "HAMBURG: End of the line. Be sure to gather all your possessions. Prepare to leave the car on the left. You will find Mr. Holdstein in the station. He will give you instructions as to where you can find food and lodging. Keep your family together; watch the smaller children lest they get lost in the crowd."

Mr. Epp and Mr. Franzen were called by the conductor to follow him to the railcar at the end of the train. There seemed to be a problem with one of the passengers in that car. Upon arriving there, they found Mrs. Sperling hysterical. Finally she explained to them through her sobs and gasps that her husband had died suddenly the day before. She hadn't known where to turn, and her grown sons suggested she do nothing until they came to Hamburg. The conductor was angry that she had not reported the death the day before since now he would have to deal with the legal matters. With the assistance of some of the other elders, they finally appeased the officials, and arrangements were made for an impromptu funeral. In a strange land, Mrs. Sperling, with her family of nine – from age twenty-four to five months – said goodbye to the husband and father. Having suffered a devastating loss herself, Elizabeth Fast and Catherine Sperling began a lifelong friendship. The entire group of Mennonites were mourning this loss and wondering what other calamity would come to them before they reached that "Promised Land."

What a mass of people moving slowly to the enormous building! Although they kept shuffling forward, they could not help but gaze with wonder at the enormous buildings all around them. Never had they seen the like! So many trains were chugging down different tracks, their whistles sounding and their steam being released at intervals to the amazement of all.

After much standing in line while papers and baggage were checked and rechecked, the travelers were directed to the building across from the tracks. It was six stories high. "How will we ever climb all those steps?" wondered the travelers. This tall building would be their home until they boarded the ship. Heinrich Schuett, a Mennonite employee of the Hamburg American Line, was very helpful in assisting them in moving through the port.

Here they exchanged their money from Russian rubles to American dollars.

The women found a common kitchen where they set about cooking some *Borscht*, their preferred comfort food. It would be a welcome change from the sausage, *Tvaebuck* and dried fruit they had eaten for the last week. They also bought flour and milk to mix up big batches of *Tvaebuck* for the long ocean journey. Laundry facilities were also available, and great heaps of dirty clothes were once again clean and packed carefully in the various bundles. Those with babies in diapers bemoaned the fact that it had been so difficult to even rinse soiled diapers during the long train journey. They wondered what kind of facilities they would find onboard the ship. They hoped the ship's facilities would prove better than those of the train, where wet diapers had been rinsed in a common bucket and hung to dry over the back of their seats. Along with the discomfort everyone endured, more than one baby had suffered diaper rash.

The children were fascinated by all the hustle and bustle of the big city. The older ones were constantly reminded to keep watch over the little ones.

The older men and boys were busy unloading their possessions from the freight cars. Under the watchful eyes of mothers and wives, their possessions were sorted and repacked. There were things they would need on the ocean voyage that now needed to be repacked into their personal bundles. The young men and boys watched as working men wrestled the crates and chests and heavy equipment onto wagons to be pulled up the long gangplank and into the ship's hold. Everyone hoped that his or her possessions would be placed in the right ship. There were so many huge ships in the harbor!

It came as no surprise when the news was announced that Mr. and Mrs. Adam Schmidt had changed their mind about immigrating. They made the complicated arrangements to return to Klippenfeld. They had been less than enthusiastic throughout the trip so far, and when Mrs. Schmidt saw the ships and imagined the endless water of the Atlantic, she panicked. Mr. Schmidt, too, had been uneasy about this voyage and readily agreed with her demands to return to the home they had known so long. Elder Epp reminded them about the warning in the scripture that he who sets his face to the plow should not turn back. Still, they could not be persuaded to continue. There were others that were tempted to turn back but stoically determined to continue on this perilous venture. The Schmidts found a local couple who were willing at this short notice to buy their sailing tickets. The couple hurriedly packed their meager possessions and joined the

Mennonite group that now numbered nine hundred and eighty souls, counting infants and children.

Heinrich Schuett was a great help since he could speak both the High German and the low dialect. As they lined up to purchase the tickets for the ocean voyage, decisions again had to be made. Should they spend the extra money to get good accommodations on the ship, or should they endure further discomfort in the cheaper area? Mr. Schuett suggested that the elderly and those with young children should buy the more expensive accommodations, while the young men and women could sleep in the dormitory-like area. They could easily spend their days in the common area or on deck, or even crowd in with their families in the small staterooms.

Again excitement and anxiety dueled as the day for embarkation arrived.

The line formed, and slowly those who accepted the hardships of daily living moved forward toward the gangplank that would permanently separate them from the life they had known.

To their surprise, they found the accommodations aboard *The Teutonia* quite comfortable. Each family had its own little cabin, with beds that looked like bins attached to the wall. Each bunk had a pad about two inches thick to serve as a mattress. This would feel luxurious after the hard wooden seats of the trains. The children were excited to be able to sleep in the bin above their parents. Parents were thankful for the side barriers to the bunks so no one would roll out of bed should the ship roll. The ceilings were low, and it took a few bumps before the taller men remembered to duck their heads in the otherwise comfortable accommodations.

The dorm accommodations had even lower ceilings, but otherwise were equipped like the cabins above them.

The voyagers made themselves as comfortable as possible. Feather ticks and quilts had been placed over the meager mattresses. The cabin took on a cozy atmosphere when three long blasts from the ship's fog-horns indicated the ship was leaving the harbor. Everyone rushed to the deck to bid farewell to the homeland and to those on shore seeing them off. Many a tear fell, and many a man assured his wife that all would be well. Nevertheless, even the men had a sense of loss as the ship pulled away from the shore.

In due time, each family gathered its own and returned to its accommodations. Fathers found their way to the ship's kitchen to buy coffee for the evening meal, which would again consist of dried meat, dried fruit, and the roasted *Tvaebuck* on which they had survived for almost two weeks. Occasionally, a family would splurge and buy soup or mush in the ship's kitchen, but it wasn't very appetizing or tasty, so most were content with the provisions they themselves had brought.

Night fell shortly after the evening meal had been eaten, and even the adventuresome young adults had retired to their sleeping accommodations. The dim lanterns had been extinguished and all was quiet, save the occasional cry of a baby and the constant *thump, thump* of the steam engines as the ship made its way out into the endless Atlantic. This would be their home for the next two weeks – maybe longer.

The first two days were sunny and calm, and most of the passengers spent their days on deck. They soon tired of looking at the sea and realized the glare of the sun on the water was harmful to their eyes. Children were warned not to look at the water. They were all hopeful that the weather would continue sunny and mild. Although it became cloudy the third day, it remained warm, and they continued to enjoy the deck in preference to the dark, dingy cabins.

Everyone was content and optimistic about the trip until the night of August 22, when everyone was awakened by the loud clanging of the ship's bell. A sailor came running through the narrow hallways shouting, "FIRE! FIRE! FIRE! ALL ON DECK! CAPTAIN'S ORDERS!"

How they hustled, wrapping the younger ones in blankets, and urging older ones to put on their clothing as well as their coats quickly. Fathers grabbed their money belts and strapped them around their waists even as they pulled up their trousers and stepped into their boots. As the sailor came through again, urging them to hurry, Father asked if the lower deck had been warned.

"Yes, they are already getting to the deck," called the sailor without even stopping.

"Katharina, can you manage the children? I must go warn and help Mrs. Fast as well as Mrs. Sperling. They will no doubt need help," called Hoinz.

But when he reached their door the two widows already had their youngsters in tow and were carrying the babies snugly wrapped in warm blankets. Hoinz assisted first one and then the other up the steep stairway and then returned to his own family. Finally, the families were all gathered and accounted for. They huddled together and one and then another led the group in prayer for deliverance from the fire as they watched the black smoke billow up into the moonlit night. They were terrified that they might burn up, but at the same time they did not want to drown in the shark-infested waters. Only God could deliver them.

Soon some of the men thought they might join the bucket brigade that was hoisting buckets of water from the sea and sending it down below to pour onto the blaze in the boiler room. Their help was appreciated as the sailors, with the encouragement of the captain, continued this seemingly hopeless task.

Elderly Mr. Peters, who was too old to join the fire fighters, started to sing, *"So nehme meine Hände, und liefer mich aus."*[19] Others joined in with faltering voices, but the Lord heard their beseeching. The black smoke became lighter-colored steam, and at last a sailor came by to inform the crowd that the fire was under control, and they would soon be allowed to return to their beds.

"PRAISE BE TO GOD!" was heard all over the ship as mothers comforted their children and each other with this promise. It was good to get back to their cabins, but it was difficult to get back to sleep after this close call.

Morning came, however, and it was such a beautiful day that most of the passengers spent the day on deck. The conversation inevitably turned to the events of the previous night. They were in common agreement that the Lord had intervened on their behalf. Six days of their ocean journey had passed; surely the rest of the trip would be uneventful.

---

[19] "So take Thou my hand and deliver me"

Chapter Eleven

The passengers enjoyed several days of very mild weather after the night of the fire. Most of them spent a great deal of time in the fresh air on deck. New friendships were formed and others grew deeper.

Although Mrs. Fast and Mrs. Sperling were busy with their children, they, too, found time to relax on deck. Most of the other passengers had heard of their bereavement and stopped to offer condolences. It was a rare family that had not suffered loss of some kind in recent years; either children or parents had died at some time prior to the trip. Death was no stranger to any of them. They had learned to accept it with stoicism; however, the grief was there, and an occasional tear would drop as they recollected these sad memories.

On this occasion, Elizabeth Fast and Catherine Sperling were conversing about their hopes for the new country. Catherine spoke. "I want Jake and Herman to file their own claims, while I file in my late husband's name. If we can find land close together, they can help me with mine. My girls can help me, and I'm sure we can manage. Land will not always be available, so it is best to buy it while we can."

Elizabeth replied, "I hope to buy also, if I can find a place close to my parents or my brother. I want to have something for my children."

Just then Thelma and Tina Sperling came by. Seeing their mother enjoying the sunshine, they offered to take sleeping Daniel down to their cabin. Tina offered to take little Mary Fast, who was also asleep. They would watch them in the Sperling cabin until it was time for the evening meal.

Then Jake Sperling came by to see if his mother needed anything. Seeing an empty deck chair he pulled it closer and joined the conversation. He had just been visiting with one of the sailors who told him that one of the boilers had overheated, causing the fire a few nights ago. Unless it could be repaired, their progress would be slowed, and it would take another two or three days to reach New York. The captain was reluctant to have the repairs made, because they would have to use sea water to refill it, and the minerals in the sea water would ruin the boiler in time.

Elizabeth voiced her regret at that, but Jake assured her it was better to arrive safely two days late than not at all. They would just have to exercise patience. He asked about her husband, and then regretted it when he heard of his untimely death. Offering his condolences, he also offered to help her with whatever she might need when they reached land and had to deal with switching once more to train travel.

Just then Martha, Albert, Peter, and Matilda walked up. "We're hungry. Is it almost suppertime?" they asked.

Elizabeth thanked both Jake and his mother for their kindness and then rose to take her children down to prepare their supper.

Jake turned to his mother. "Is that woman really traveling alone with all those children?"

"Yes, she is. She is a strong one. She has helped me deal with your father's death in a remarkable way. I think she is a fine Christian woman. She will, no doubt, be taken by some widower who needs a woman to mother his children. If so, I hope he treats her kindly."

Nothing more was said as they, too, returned to their cabin for the evening meal. But Jake had been so impressed by the courage of this young woman that he determined to go out of his way to ease her load whenever possible.

He would speak to his sisters, Thelma and Tina and even Rachel. Surely they would be willing to help with those little ones. No wonder he had never seen her on the deck before. She was always taking care of the little ones below, and even the older two were not old enough to be trusted with the younger two on the deck.

Later that evening he saw Elizabeth on deck leaning on the rail looking out over that vast expanse of water. There were many others on deck but out of earshot. He walked over and leaned over the rail himself. After some time he spoke. "That sure is a lot of water out there."

She agreed and then added, "It sure is warm, considering it is September. Back in Russia I'm sure they have had frost."

"Yes. I spoke to one of the sailors this afternoon. He was concerned about this warm weather. He said warm weather always indicated a storm coming. But he is hoping we won't encounter any."

"The rocking of the boat is so gentle. I don't think anyone has been seasick."

"I guess being seasick can be pretty bad sometimes, but I don't think many people have ever died from it. It can be very unpleasant, though."

At this, Elizabeth excused herself, noting that she needed to check on her little ones. On her way back to the cabin she thought, *I can't believe that man talked to me. I wonder what Johann would think of that*. For a moment she felt guilty. It did seem nice to talk to a man for a change. *If he is Catherine's son, he must be a good person*, she thought.

Jake stayed on the deck for another hour with strange thoughts of his own. *She seems to be a fine woman. Mother seems to really like her. I wonder how she will fare in the new country on her own and with five children!* At last he turned and went down the steep stairs to his bunk with all the other single men.

Jake did not see Elizabeth the next day, and by the afternoon, he had decided that he would offer to go to the ship's kitchen and get her some coffee the next morning. It must be hard for her to do that with those five little ones always there. Surely she did not send her son Albert. He couldn't be more than seven years old. For a moment he thought, *I wonder how old she is. She must be in her late twenties to have five children. She doesn't look over twenty-one*. Jake shrugged his shoulders. What difference did it make? He crawled into his bunk among the other single men.

The next morning he got the coffee and knocked on her door. Albert answered the door. "Good morning," he said courteously. "What do you want? Mama is feeding little Mary."

"I just thought your mother might like some coffee with her breakfast. Would you take it to her?"

Albert took the cup with both hands, thanked him, and turned away, closing the door.

Jake turned to go back to the kitchen for some coffee for himself, but as he walked, he pictured this young woman feeding her fifth child. It was a beautiful picture he saw, and then he forced himself to think of other things. Would the storm materialize as the sailor had predicted?

The following day was Sunday, and the travelers all gathered on the deck for worship services. Their singing was joyful as they praised God for protecting them from the recent fire. They voiced their thankfulness in song and also implored God's protection for the rest of their journey. Their singing brought up even the ship's crew, for the boilers had been tended to, and the sea was calm. As the crew listened to the singing, several were reminded of a time in their youth when their mothers had sung to them some of the same songs. They stood to the side and listened.

After much singing, Elder Jantzen rose, and opening his Bible, he turned to Genesis 8. He read the account of Noah and then spoke to the crowd. "We have been on this voyage now for ten days and before that on trains for several. We had delays at various places, and I believe many of you have become weary of travel. Let me remind you of Noah and encourage you to carry on without complaining. Noah was in the ark more than a hundred days. It rained for forty of those days. I don't think it was a gentle rain. No doubt the ark rocked about to some degree. The Bible doesn't say they were seasick. Perhaps they were. We have been greatly blessed in that the seas have been calm. We have had smooth sailing, for which we thank God. But if the weather should turn bad and the seas become rough, let us still put our trust in the Almighty God, who is our refuge and strength." He spoke on about the blessings of God for some time and then led the group in more singing, ending as they had at home with the *Doxology*. This reminder of home brought a few tears, as loneliness for the familiar came to mind.

As the crowd dispersed to prepare the noon meal, they noticed a low bank of clouds ahead. After the meal the older ones and the very young settled down for a nap, but the young adults and the older children gathered once more on the deck for some socializing. The clouds looked more ominous, and the waves were increasing in size. The ship was rocking much more than they were accustomed to. It wasn't long before a sailor came by and ordered them to return to their quarters. Several sailors accompanied them, and they were soon busy collecting the deck chairs and everything that was loose on deck, tying it down.

"We are in for a gale. Let's hope it doesn't last too long. Be sure to fasten everything in your quarters. It just might move around and hit you," the sailor warned the young people as they started down the stairs.

They warned those who had been below of the coming difficulty. The boys and young men were joking about the new situation. They looked forward to some excitement after the days of boredom they had endured.

A few minutes later, a cabin boy knocked on each door and warned the occupants of the coming rough seas. He told them to keep the little ones in the bunks between adults, and to be sure to hang on to the edge of their bunks. A container was provided for possible seasickness, and it would be emptied twice a day by a member of the ship's crew. He checked the lanterns to make sure they would not come loose and cause another fire. Then he left them. Because of the early darkness, most of the passengers went to bed. Perhaps they could sleep through the storm.

But that was not to be. Before midnight the ship was lunging ahead, then dipping into the deep depressions between the waves. It seemed the cabin walls were spinning this way and that. The lantern gave its dim light as it swung to and fro with the action of the ship. They had to hang on to the edge of the bunk to keep from falling out as the ship rolled first this way and then that. The chest slid from one side of the small room to the other. There would be no sleep for anyone but the very young children in their mother's arms. One by one they tried to reach the container, only to lose their balance and slide across the floor. A few managed to reach the container in time, but most of their retching landed on the floor. The sour smell only made others seasick as well.

The rocking and rolling of the ship made the timbers moan and groan, and many of the passengers were wondering if this would be their end. Had they come this far only to perish in a watery grave? They cried out to their God for mercy, but the storm raged on.

When morning finally came, a few brave ones attempted to get to the ship's kitchen for some coffee, only to find the kitchen closed because of the storm. They stumbled back to their quarters, bouncing from one wall of the narrow passageway to the other.

In the Epp cabin, Katharina hugged Anna and Margaret to her bosom while Father held Johann and Peter.

When there was a brief lull in the storm, Katharina turned to her husband and said, "*Voah vie daught mocha?*"[20]

Father replied, "*Vun Gott vilt.*[21] We must trust Him." Then he started to sing, "Only Trust Him, Only Trust Him." To his great surprise this seemed to lessen his nausea, and he encouraged his wife to join him.

In one of the very small cabins Nick and Anna Thiezen were trying to encourage each other. Nick was having a very bad time with nausea. Anna was holding his head as he emptied the contents of his stomach into the receptacle provided. During a pause while

---

[20] *Werden wir dat henkriege?* Will we make it?
[21] *Wenn Gott es will*, or If God wills.

he caught his breath, Anna began to feel sick. Just at that moment the ship took a sudden roll to the left, and Anna was thrown against the side of their chest. She winced at the blow and then crept to her bunk. Maybe if she lay down the nausea would leave her.

In the women's dorm there was much screaming and retching as well. Maria was praying. As she reached into her pinafore pocket for a handkerchief to cover her mouth, she felt the wooden bird Karl had given her. *I don't suppose I'll ever see you again, Karl,* she thought to herself. *I had hoped that maybe someday you and I would marry, but now I don't think it will happen.*

In the men's quarters, Hoinz was thinking of his little Lena. He hoped she was not suffering seasickness like so many others were.

Similar episodes took place in various areas of the ship. But the storm raged on through another night. Thankfully, at about noon of the second day, quite suddenly, the ship stopped its lunging and rolling, everything settled down.

Those that were able began immediately to clean up the mess. They would have to do a lot of laundry. Hopefully there would be enough water to wash the many sheets that had had to absorb so much of their seasickness. How would they get rid of the smell?

They managed somehow, but the odor remained. It was almost enough to make the nausea return, so as much as possible, they stayed on the open deck.

Chapter Twelve

After the calm had returned, Katie noticed she hadn't seen either Nick or Anna Thiezen since before the storm. She asked her mother, "Have you seen the Thiezens since the storm? They were at the church service, but I haven't seen them since."

Just then they heard the ship's bell sound and soon heard footsteps in the hallway. Someone was calling an alarm. "Is there a doctor around, or a midwife? We need a doctor NOW!"

Katharina opened the cabin door and saw Nick Thiezen. He was distraught. "Oh, Katharina! Do you know of a doctor on the ship?"

"No, I don't. But how can I help you?"

"It's Anna. I think her time has come, but it is too early. She is very sick and in great pain."

Katharina came rushing to the cabin door. She told Katie to rush up to the deck and get her father to find a doctor. She herself went back with Nick to see poor Anna.

With soothing words she consoled Anna and offered her some water to drink. "Please, relax my dear. The pain will subside if you can just relax."

By then Hoinz was at the door with Dr. Toews. The doctor took over, and Hoinz and Katharina left to join the crowd on deck to pray for their dear friend Anna, ending with, "Thy will be done." They knew full well what the outcome might be. But surely Anna's life would be spared. She was so young and her whole life lay before her.

After what seemed like hours, the doctor came up on deck. Sorrowfully, he walked over to the group and announced, "We tried to save her, but we just were not able to. The little boy came too soon. He gave one feeble cry and then was gone. And poor Mrs. Thiezen died about half an hour later. I was unable to stop the hemorrhaging." The doctor put his hands to his face, grieving the loss of his patient. He suggested someone go to the grieving husband.

Hoinz and Katharina immediately left to bring what comfort they could to poor Nick. The captain of *The Teutonia* was notified, and he ordered some of the crew to prepare for the burial. Katharina asked for help to prepare the bodies. Mrs. Sperling and Mrs. Fast soon appeared. They understood grief.

"*Ach!* Such a lovely lady!" Elizabeth Fast commented as she bathed the departed sister.

And Catherine Sperling replied, "Yes, and look at this tiny little boy! See those tiny feet and fingers; the nails are not yet formed."

With flowing tears they completed their task, and then Elizabeth said, "Wait just a minute. I must get something." She left but soon returned with a delicately crocheted blanket. "Here. Wrap this around the little boy's body. My Mary doesn't need this anymore."

Anna was dressed in what had been her wedding dress just two years before. The little boy was wrapped gently in the lacey blanket and laid on his mother's breast.

Hoinz, meanwhile, had notified the church members, and they were already assembled on deck. The seamen came, and against Nick's urgent protests, they wrapped the body of his dear wife in a heavy canvas. The law demanded she be buried at sea. Hoinz led the poor man away as the sailors carried the body down the long hallway and up the stairs where the solemn congregation was gathered.

Flanked by his closest friends, Abe Penner and Will Quiring, Nick walked slowly, grieving the loss of his wife, behind the makeshift coffin. The crowd parted to let them through to the railing of the ship. There the body was laid on a row of chairs and Elder Nuefeldt stood to pray. He spoke for a few minutes, quoting from II Corinthians 5: "Therefore we are always confident, knowing that, whilst we are at home in the body, we are absent from the Lord, for we walk by faith, not by sight." The congregation sang "Safe in the Arms of Jesus," and the congregation was dismissed.

Will and Abe persuaded Nick to return to their cabin while the body was reverently dropped into the sea.

The voyage continued without incident, and a few days later, the travelers heard that welcome call: "Land Ho!" It brought everyone up to the deck, and there was much cheerful rejoicing. The immigrants gathered, and Elder Nuefeldt offered thanks to God for the safe voyage.

The captain came on deck and announced to the excited crowd that it would be at least another day and a half before they would be anchored, and then it might well be another day before they would disembark. He thanked them for choosing to sail with *The Teutonia* and told them if any decided to go back to Hamburg, the ship would leave for the return trip in two weeks.

The crowd refused to leave the ship's rail. They were fascinated by the sight of land, even though it was just a little line of discoloration on the western horizon. As they watched, it did appear to grow more prominent. At last they realized it was time for the evening meal. Mothers persuaded their families to return to their quarters.

In a few days they would be on solid ground. They would have a hot meal after two weeks of salted pork, *Tvaebuck* and dried fruit. It was hard for anyone to sleep that night. Soon they would reach their dream, even if it meant another five-day train ride.

The next morning, even before daylight, many were again on deck. Now they could see outlines of buildings. They were as high as those they had seen in Hamburg. This was no wilderness. This was civilization!

And then they saw a smaller boat coming up to their ship. A nearby sailor explained that this was the harbor pilot. It was a complicated task to take the big ocean-going vessel into the harbor, so each harbor had captains who knew every inch of the harbor and so were able to guide the big ship safely to the dock.

Then what a hustle and bustle! Mothers gathered their children for a final wash-up. Clothing was changed so they would look presentable when they stepped on solid ground once more. Belongings were gathered and stashed into bundles. Older children were given bundles to be responsible for and were told to take the hands of their younger siblings. "Now stay together!" was heard over and over. But at last the crowd in the gangway began to move. They were about to step on solid ground after seventeen days at sea.

The captain and several of the crew members were lined up near the debarkation gate. They warned the eager passengers to be very careful as they left the gate, because it would seem strange to walk on solid ground after being aboard the ship so long.

Even with the warning, many stumbled, and a few fell as their wobbly legs met solid ground. Embarrassed, but not hurt, they rose and stumbled on.

They were surprised to be greeted by a committee of three who had come all the way from Nebraska to welcome them and help them through the complicated immigration procedures. David Goertz, Wilhelm Ewert, and Cornelius Jantzen spoke good English, and having gone through the procedure just a year or so before, they knew just what to do. This greatly benefited the weary travelers.

They were taken to housing built especially for immigrants, and after a two-day delay, were lined up to go through the immigration and health checks. They were required to step over a low footstool, where a white-haired doctor determined if they were healthy enough to be accepted into the country. Only a few elderly were ordered to step aside, but upon further examination and the assurance that they had family members with them who would care for their needs, they too were passed along.

Castle Gardens Hotel proved to be a comfortable place for them to relax while waiting for the business matters to be conducted. All foreign money needed to be exchanged for American money. And some supplies needed to be purchased for the long journey by train that awaited them. They had not anticipated the luxurious accommodations. Oh! How good it felt to slip into a real bed with clean sheets and pillowcases.

While they were waiting for all the necessary arrangements to be made, Jake and Herman Sperling decided to do a little exploring in the big city. Immediately their sisters, Thelma and Tina, expressed a desire to go with them.

Mrs. Sperling would have to appear before the immigration officials, so she did not want to be bothered with the little ones. So the older children offered to take them along. Just as they were ready to start out, they saw Mrs. Fast with her five. Jake turned to her and asked if the older two might like to go along on their little jaunt. So it was quite a group that headed up the street to see what they would see. After walking five blocks, they came to a section of shops. The girls were interested in looking at the clothing and millinery shops, so the boys walked on, promising to meet them in front of the store in one hour. What a time they had at the great displays of material! They marveled at the velvets and satins on display in all the colors of the rainbow. The bonnets, too, were beyond their highest dreams. Never had they seen such finery. They were amazed at the lace and fancy feathers that adorned those bonnets. In their dreams they each chose the fabric of their choice, knowing full well they would never have it. Thelma, the oldest, was the first to speak. "We shouldn't even be looking at these goods. It surely is sinful to think of such frivolous adornment. Mother would be shocked to see us here." With a tinge of guilt and disappointment, they sadly retraced their steps to meet their brothers and return to the Castle Gardens Hotel.

The boys, too, were impressed with all the shops, but even more impressed by the traffic. Beautiful horses were pulling fancy buggies and even some carriages with six seats. Jake vowed under his breath that one day he would own a team of matched horses and would have a carriage equally fancy.

Albert Fast, who was holding on to Jake's hand, pointed out a matched team pulling a white carriage and said, "When I get big, I'm going to buy Mama a team like that, and a carriage, too!"

At a shop nearby they saw toys of all kinds. On impulse, Jake bought a little stick horse similar to the one Albert had pointed to. Giving it to Albert, he said, "Here. You can pretend this is one of the horses until you get big."

Other penny gifts were purchased for the little ones. They rationalized that the gifts were needed to keep the children entertained on the long train ride awaiting them.

Thelma and Tina questioned Jake about the package he kept hidden behind him, but he would not divulge its contents. Later that evening, they noticed that Mrs. Fast had a new comb holding her long hair in the bun at the nape of her neck.

"Do you suppose Jake got that for her?" Tina whispered to her older sister. "I noticed that he has been paying attention to her lately."

Thelma replied, "I wouldn't be surprised. I see him looking at her so often. When she looks at him, he turns and his face gets red."

That evening was another special occasion. The group would part, as many of them would board a train for Canada. Close friendships had been formed onboard the ship, and now it was time to say goodbye. With much fondness, farewells were said. After the meal, Elder Nuefeldt suggested they sing the favorite, "God Be with You Till We Meet Again." The singing was sincere, but voices broke as the thought of parting came to each.

They were again pleasantly surprised the next day when they boarded the train that was to take them on the final part of their long journey. The seats were cushioned and covered with plush red material. Mothers cautioned their children to be careful not to soil the beautiful seat covers.

At last they heard that welcome sound, "ALL ABOARD!" and then the slow *chug, chug* as the engines began pulling them toward their new home.

Chapter Thirteen

The train rumbled along with the passengers eagerly looking out the window to see this new country they would soon call home. After they left the smoking factories and other industrial areas, they came to streets and streets of fine houses. More than one immigrant wondered if he or she would ever live in fine houses like those they saw.

The younger men vowed they would someday build houses like that for the young women they hoped to marry. But how they would get the lumber they did not know, for they had learned that Nebraska had no trees. Would they find material that could be made into bricks?

Night time came, and the passengers slept comfortably in the red velvet-covered seats.

In the morning they found the landscape had changed. Now they saw trees in every direction, with only small villages interrupting the view. The train made stops at most of these villages, where strangers boarded the train. They spoke pleasantly to the immigrants, but of course they did not speak German, so the communication was mostly smiles. A few of the immigrants had picked up some English on the trip, as most of the sailors had used that language.

By late afternoon, several of the more sociable had learned a bit more of the language. Early the next morning they reached Pittsburgh. They would have to change trains there for Chicago. Realizing they would have a three-hour wait, many again explored the city. They were reminded of the rivers back home in Russia as they saw the Ohio, the Allegheny, and the Monongahela come together. What a lot of water!

Mrs. Sperling mentioned that she would like to see some of the shops near the depot. With Thelma and Tina staying with the younger children, she started out with her friend Mrs. Fast. After walking a few blocks, they ran into Jake and Herman, who had also decided to explore this bustling metropolis. Seeing a hotel with an inviting restaurant nearby, they decided to splurge and have coffee and some dessert. It was somewhat difficult to communicate with the waitress, but they finally pointed to a fluffy yellow confection that the people at another table were having. The waitress understood and brought them their first piece of lemon meringue pie along with a little language lesson on how to say the name of this sweet dessert. Then it was back to the station to wait for the train for Chicago. Others, too, had ventured out, if for no other reason than to stretch their legs. So it was that they walked back to the station with quite a few of their acquaintances, Katie, Maria, Cornelius, and Abraham Epp among them. Abraham was especially proud of his acquisition of the English language and was eager to practice it. They all laughed heartily as they tried to pronounce that strange name, Monongahela.

Boarding the train that afternoon, they realized they would be crossing that wide river. They saw the bridge looming before them. Would it be strong enough for that heavy train to cross? There were no railings on the bridge and quite a few passengers hid their eyes as the train swayed this way and that. But they crossed safely and soon the landscape changed again. Now they saw open fields with farmers working to bring in the harvest of corn, a crop new to them.

Another train change in the busy station at Chicago, and at last they were on the final leg of their trip. Again they lost a sizeable number from their group: some left the group to go to Southern Minnesota, and a good number headed to South Dakota. Sad good-byes were again said, and it was a group of ninety families that got on the train headed for Nebraska. A sense of anticipation swept through the crowd. They crossed the Mississippi soon after leaving Chicago and headed across Iowa. Prosperous farms were seen on both sides of the track, along with many groves of a variety of trees. The weary travelers were getting excited about the future possibilities. They had only one more river to cross: that was the Missouri. Again the high bridge had no side walls, and many looked the other way, fear gripping their hearts as the train swayed from side to side while the engine slowed for the high trestle.

Hoinz and Katharina Epp were careful to speak words of encouragement to those who had suffered loss during the trip, assuring Elizabeth Fast that they would help her reach her family. Catherine Sperling depended on her grown sons to help her get settled. Nick Thiezen looked so forlorn that Cornelius and Katie moved up to sit beside him. Cornelius tried to encourage him by pointing out the possibilities of the new country. Perhaps they would find land close together, and they could go fishing together after they had built their houses. The elder Hoinz came walking by and asked if Nick would be willing to help build their house. Hoinz promised he could shelter with them through the winter. Then, in the spring, they would in turn help him build a house on his own land.

"What is the use?" Nick replied. "All my hopes were buried in the ocean."

To which Katharina replied, "Now, now. Don't give up. There will be good days ahead. Just trust in God. He gives, and He takes away, but He is always good. There is hope for the future."

The three men who had met them in New York were also there to offer encouragement. They had been busy throughout the train trip, explaining to the travelers some of the conditions they could expect in this new country, as well as trying to teach them enough English so they would be able to deal with the railroad land agents that would be selling them this rich Nebraska farmland.

Chug, chug, chug, a loud hiss of steam, and a long mournful whistle at last told them they were approaching the end of their journey. The conductor came through their car and announced the approaching station. "Liiiiiiiincoooooln," he called out. "Be sure you collect all your belongings. Watch the children. There are many trains switching here. The depot is toward the front of the train. There are assistants in the depot to help you. They will tell you where you can retrieve the freight you shipped from Chicago."

A brakeman was stationed at the exit of each car to help the ladies and children down the short flight of stairs. Again their legs felt wobbly, but they managed to get into the depot without a problem. What a busy place!

They looked for the station master and then saw a special desk set up with a sign reading, "Immigrants." *En masse* they moved toward the sign. They were directed down the street to a large building with the sign "Immigrant House." The railroad had built it hurriedly to accommodate those coming through. Construction workers were still up on the roof getting the last shingles over the new wing.

Each family was directed to a separate room. These rooms were not large enough to accommodate some of the larger families, so the older children were given access to two dormitory rooms, one at the east end of the building for the ladies, and one at the west end for the gentlemen, where double-decked bunks greeted them. These accommodations were greatly appreciated. They fully realized that for several months they would not have luxurious shelter.

The men were busy dealing with local merchants who tried to sell them everything from plows, mowers, and wagons, to every kind of farm animal. Hoinz Epp discussed the matter with his sons. They agreed that they would wait until they reached their destination. Surely those who had settled here some years ago might have equipment they would be willing to loan. If not, they could return to Lincoln to purchase what they needed. It was only a day's journey.

Again the crowd separated, forty families choosing to travel on to Kansas, where previous Mennonite families had settled.

Of the nine hundred eighty souls that had traveled *The Teutonia*, only thirty-five families now set out on the local train to Sutton, Nebraska. Among them were the Hoinz Epps, the Ben Franzen family, the Nuefeldts, the Isaac Penners, Jantzens, Remples, Pankratz, Bergens, Freish, Ziebets, Kroekers, Thiezens, Quirings, and Nick Fast. Six freight cars with all their belongings followed them. The residents of Sutton welcomed them and made arrangements for them to spend the night. They were housed in empty grain bins, warehouses, and wherever space could be found under a roof. Many of the men and boys slept under the stars wrapped in blankets they had brought with them. It was a cold night, and they thought of the good accommodations they had had in Lincoln, but they were near their destination and were willing to endure this bit of discomfort. Tomorrow they would assemble their wagons and travel the few miles north and east to where the land had been reserved for them.

Perhaps they would find hospitality with the Mennonites who had settled on government land a few years before. Most of the travelers had a relative or friend that they could count on.

However, when they reached their final destination and encountered their acquaintances, the welcome was quite reserved. "We are happy to see you, but we are fearful for the winter. We experienced an infestation of grasshoppers this past summer. We fear we may not have enough grain to feed our animals, and still save some for seed."

Most of the travelers did find a place to sleep with relatives or acquaintances. The remainder found shelter at a crude immigrant house that had been erected hastily near the little town of Henderson.

The next day the men were met with several representatives of the Burlington Railroad Company with horses and buggies to take the settlers to the various properties that had been reserved for them. Their wives gathered at the immigrant house, doing laundry, mending, and caring for the needs of the children. They were happy to have plenty of water and lye soap as well as clotheslines on which to hang their wet things. Children were lined up to have baths, and dried prunes were cooked with milk donated by the nearby settlers. Tonight they would have a good hot meal, with the *Plumamos*, ham, and fresh *Tvaebuck*.

As the sun went down, the mothers and wives were eagerly awaiting the return of the men and their report as to the land they had purchased.

Hoinz and his three older sons, Hoinz, Cornelius, and Abraham, and Nick Thiezen were enthusiastic. They had found a half section of land with a creek running through the middle. The grass along the creek was waist high, while the upland was covered with buffalo grass. This would be ideal for the sod houses they planned to build.

Mrs. Sperling and her sons had agreed to buy the other half section. They would build their houses close together and be able to exchange work. Things were working out well. They had stopped at the Abe Heinrichs', who lived next to this section, and bought a team of oxen with a breaking plow. Heinrichs had finished plowing this grass-covered virgin soil and would do all his future work with horses. The men could hardly wait for morning, they were so eager to get started.

Mrs. Fast had met up with her family. They would help her find some suitable land near their place the next day.

Chapter Fourteen

Long before daybreak, the men were up and eager to get started on what would be a long day of back-breaking work. The women had also been up early, fixing coffee and porridge for their breakfast. They tied up bundles of *Tvaebuck* and some of the dwindling supply of dried fruit for their lunch, as well as a jug of fresh water from the well nearby.

It was hard labor for the men who had been traveling so long with no physical activity, but their enthusiasm and sheer necessity kept them going. They had decided they would dig down a bit to see if they could find a clay base for the floor. That would be easier to maintain, and digging down a bit would also provide greater warmth for the coming winter. So they dug. The oxen seemed incredibly slow to the men, who had been used to working with horses. They realized that breaking up this land was very hard work, so they patiently urged the oxen onward.

The men took turns with the oxen, while the others dug up the grass and turned over the rich black soil until they came to more yellowish dirt. They were thrilled to see the depth of the topsoil. Crops would flourish here.

By noon they had excavated an area 48 feet by 24 feet. This, they thought, should be enough to begin with. The afternoon was spent digging and cutting the sod into sections for the walls. These building blocks were three feet long and two-and-a-half feet wide, as had been recommended by previous builders. They worked until it was too dark to see. Wearily they returned to the immigrant house, pleased with their accomplishment but aching in every joint and muscle.

The women had a hearty meal ready for them. The children were already sleeping. "What did you get done?" was the question from many a wife and mother.

Too tired to talk much, they said, "Not enough, but we will work again tomorrow."

And so the days continued. Work stopped for Sunday, and the church service held in the crowded building was well attended. Pastor Unruh preached an encouraging sermon but also warned of dangers that might assail them. He referred to II Corinthians 6:17: *Wherefore come out from among them, and be ye separate.* "We must remember what our fathers told us. In this new country, we will encounter Englisha[22] that do not believe as we do. Although we have to sometimes do business with them, we must not accept their ways." The women listened intently, but most of the men, having done such strenuous work all week, nodded and slept, even though they felt an occasional elbow jab from the women beside them.

By Tuesday, the walls were up, and the younger Hoinz, Cornelius, and Abraham were instructed to cut the tall grass along the creek, while the elder Hoinz and Nick Thiezen walked to Sutton. They planned to buy lumber and windows, plus a door to finish the building. Surely they could hire someone in Sutton with a wagon to deliver the material to the building site. By Friday they had laid rough boards

---

[22] Mennonites in America referred to non-Mennonites, most of whom spoke English, as "Englisha."

for the ceiling and put up rafters for the roof. They continued to work long hours on Saturday, and after church on Sunday, they would take their families out to show them their accomplishment.

Excitement ran high among all the settlers. The women were dubious about living in dirt homes but tried not to show their feelings, since the men had worked so hard.

"There it is!" Cornelius stood and pointed, and in the distance they could see a break in the endless waving grasses.

Hoinz helped Katharina down from the wagon and walked proudly to the doorway. "See? I bought a door and some windows, so we will have light. The ceiling is lumber, as is the roof, but we covered the roof also with this long grass to help shed the rain." Then, seeing her disconsolate face, he added, "This is only for a start. After we have a good wheat crop, I will build you a fine house, better than what we had in Russia."

The building was long with a dividing wall in the middle. The attic was divided into two areas. On the one side the older boys could sleep, and on the other, the girls.

Katharina could see she had no choice but to accept these arrangements to shelter her family, so she tried desperately to appear pleased. She would have to make the best of this. Hopefully, it would be temporary. She encouraged her daughters to be optimistic as well. And so they mounted the wagon to return to the immigrant house, where they shared their feelings with the other women who had experienced similar disappointment.

Monday was moving-in day. This brought about a degree of excitement and enthusiasm. Today they would see how their possessions had survived the long arduous journey.

The ticking which had been filled with goose down in Russia now needed to be filled with something. Katharina did not relish the thought of sleeping on the hard boards, even though she did appreciate the crude bed that Hoinz had fashioned at one end of the dwelling. Proudly he showed her how a lower bed could be pulled out from under this. Peter, Johann, and Anna could sleep here close to their parents. Margaret, Maria, and Katie would sleep at one end of the attic, while Hoinz, Cornelius, Abraham, and Mr. Thiezen would bed down at the other end. This would keep them safe and warm through this first winter. The other end of the building would provide shelter for the oxen and other animals they might acquire. But now the important thing was to get those tickings filled with something. Hoinz had the answer, and he was soon busy with the men scything the tall grass along the creek. Piles of the long grass soon appeared at the doorway, and the women of the household were busy stuffing it into the bags made for it.

Katharina came across the wooden box built especially for her porcelain tea set. "Heaven be praised!" she exclaimed. "It is not broken. But where will I put this in this primitive abode?" She carefully placed it back in the box. It would stay there for the time being. Cautiously, she pried open the box in which the fancy lamp had been packed. Miraculously, it, too, had arrived safely. Now if she could find the container with the kerosene, she would light up this abode, dark and dingy, even though it was only mid-afternoon.

By nightfall, sufficient progress had been made, and the loads of grass had provided a degree of comfort to those who wished to have a restful night.

As they gathered around the supper table, a feeling of comfort and safety permeated the minds of even the most skeptical. This was their home. It was not a castle, but it was warm and comfortable.

The next day Father put together the *Klietaschope*, and clothing was hung in it. The place did have a semblance of home.

Now the men were busy preparing the field for the crops to be planted in the spring. Mr. Classen had offered some seed corn in exchange for the coveted red winter wheat seed that the travelers had brought from Russia. It was too late in the season to plant the winter wheat, but they carefully stored enough to be planted next fall. They would plant oats, rye, and corn in the spring. The seeds for the garden were also put in a safe place. Now if only spring would come quickly.

Katharina decided if the girls could hurry with the housework in the morning, they would all walk the half mile to where the Sperlings had settled.

Surely they would have completed their shelter by now. "We must make sure that our neighbors are taken care of," said Mother.

It was with dismay that they approached the dwelling of poor Mrs. Sperling. It was just a door into the side of the creek bank. *My goodness,* thought Katharina, *did they really need to live like animals in a hole in the ground?* As they came closer they heard the sound of Mrs. Sperling and her girls, Thelma, Tina, and Rachel, singing

Oh, they tell me of a home far beyond the skies.
Oh, they tell me of a home far away.
Oh, they tell me of a home where no storm clouds rise.
Oh, they tell me of an unclouded day.

At the knock the singing stopped, and Mrs. Sperling called out, "Come in, come in." Soon the door opened, and Katharina Epp entered with her children. Mrs. Sperling was busy cleaning the lamp chimneys while her daughters were busy cleaning the cluttered area that was obviously the kitchen of this hole in the ground.

Katharina exclaimed, "How can you sing in this situation? I thought our soddy was dismal, but this is worse."

"Now, now, let's not complain. The Good Lord has brought us here safely. We are healthy and have enough to eat. The girls and I find that if we sing, it helps us to remember that this is not really our home. We are here but for a little while. Our home is in heaven, where my dear husband has already arrived."

Just then her baby Daniel started crying and she excused herself to pick him up and nurse him. As their eyes got used to the dim light in the room, they could see that it was not quite the hole in the ground of their first impression. A canvas provided a ceiling over most of the room, and another covered the entire floor except the section where the beds stood.

Mrs. Sperling spoke again. "My boys are busy breaking the sod for the spring crops, as I suppose your men are doing as well." Then she turned to her daughter Thelma. "Now go fix some coffee. Rachel, you go and bring in some more of that twisted grass from outside so the fire doesn't go out." With her baby now satisfied, she pulled out her enamel cups and found a few pieces of leftover bread. She sprinkled a little brown sugar on the bread and said, "Now come to the table. We can visit better when we have something to eat." Over the protests of Katharina and her girls, she insisted that they share the meager fare. They had a lively visit, and only once, as Mrs. Sperling mentioned her late husband and how he would have loved to be here with them, did she shed a tear. Wiping it away quickly, she continued, "But I have my big boys. They are working hard, and soon enough we will be better off."

All too soon it was time to go home to prepare supper for their menfolk. But on the way home Mother spoke to her girls. "In my heart I have been complaining about our situation, but I will do it no more. If that woman can sing away her troubles, I think we should do the same." The girls agreed, and it was with new enthusiasm that they reached their home and prepared what food they had for the family.

Everyone was happy when Sunday came again. They got up early, and wearing the best they had, the whole family piled into the wagon to go to church at the immigrant house in Henderson. It seemed the oxen felt it was a day of rest for them, too, and they were extremely slow-moving, but Father goaded them into action, and at last they reached their destination.

How happy they were to see their friends, and what a change they noticed in the surroundings. Several houses had been started and were in various stages of being completed.

The service seemed long, but they were all attentive. They really enjoyed the singing again. Pastor Unruh announced a meeting for the men after the service. Another song was sung, and the service was over. The women gathered in the sunshine outside, waiting for the men to finish. This was a good time for them to visit, and, in spite of tired children, they did a lot of talking. They tried to put a hopeful face on their dismal conditions.

Mrs. Sperling was happy to see her friend Mrs. Fast, who reported that she was managing quite well. Her parents and siblings had welcomed her, and she had arranged to buy some land near them. She would stay with her family until spring. Then Mrs. Friesha walked up to them and asked if Mrs. Sperling could spare her daughter Thelma for a few weeks. Her baby was due anytime now, and she really needed help with her other three. It would definitely ease the crowding in the Sperling home, so Mrs. Sperling readily agreed.

Mrs. Kroeker spoke to Katharina. "I see you have grown-up daughters. I wonder if one of them could come live with us for awhile. I really could use some help with my children. I would be willing to pay her a dollar a week." And so it was arranged. Mrs. Kroeker offered to drive out to their place that afternoon to pick her up. It would be no trouble. She had a horse and buggy.

Meanwhile, the men had an interesting meeting inside the building. Mr. Kroeker led the discussion. He announced that it was time they considered building a church. The community was growing, and although the Englisha in the area had a church, it was not in harmony with the Mennonite beliefs. "We need our own church building. Otherwise, before we know it, our people will be attending that church, and we will be the losers." The majority agreed, and arrangements were made to purchase material. Those who could not afford to help pay for materials could help in the building. "We have enough men that can handle a hammer and saw, so we can get started," said Mr. Kroeker. After this was agreed on, he brought up another matter. "I have been in contact with the Fremont, Elkhorn, and Missouri Valley Railroad Company. If we can get the signatures of fifty land owners in this area, they will extend their tracks through here. And if they get signatures of those settlers west of here, the tracks will continue to Grand Island. This would be a tremendous boost to our community. We could have lumber and farm equipment brought right here to Henderson, and when we harvest our crops, we would have a much bigger market. I can see our wheat being shipped as far east

as Chicago! In addition to these advantages, we could have employment for our men through the winter and whenever they have time
through the spring and summer. It takes a lot of manpower to build
the grade and lay the tracks."

It didn't take long for the signing to take place, and the meeting
was adjourned.

The men rejoined their patient wives much more optimistic than
they had been earlier that morning. They would possibly have a
source of income for the next months, and in the long run, they would
prosper from this endeavor.

Chapter Fifteen

At the Sperling house that noon the conversation was animated. Jake was ecstatic. He would work for that railroad and earn money. Maybe by spring he would have something to offer Elizabeth Fast. Though he cast many a glance in her direction at the church services, he dared not speak to her of his heart, for he had nothing to offer her. Elizabeth needed someone to help her with those five children, and he would like to be the one to do it. He had been pleased at the friendliness her older children had shown to him in New York. He would like to teach Albert the ways of farming. And perhaps, in time, they would have other children together. He dreamed on until at last his mother spoke to him.

"Jake, would you please help Willie with his meat? He is having trouble cutting it." His mother knew he was day dreaming, and she sensed that it might be about the railroad job. *Or could it be that young widow?* she wondered.

"Sorry," he replied. "I guess my mind was elsewhere. Here, Willie. Let me help you."

"And where might your mind have been?" asked his mother.

"If you don't object, I would like to apply for work on the railroad, when we get the sod busting done, of course."

"I have no objection to that. We will need to buy some flour before spring and other things too. The weather is getting colder. Soon the children will need to wear shoes. I noticed when we got ready for church this morning that every one of the children had trouble getting their shoes on. We will pass them down, of course, but we will need a new pair. Your boots will still fit, but the way you work, they will wear out by spring. I think we need to go see Heinrich Penner. His son Heinrich is a shoemaker. Maybe he will make a pair for Rachel. Then everyone will have warm feet."

Jake's heart fell. He had figured he would use his pay to buy land for himself. He realized, of course, the needs of his family. Since his father was gone, he had to be responsible for them.

"Let's not count our chickens before they hatch," his mother continued. "The railroad may not come at all. My! How I wish we had some chickens and some eggs. I'm sorry, I should not be complaining. I should be thankful for what we have. We will see what will happen if the railroad comes."

Now Herman spoke up. "I saw some birds that look almost like the chickens we had in Russia. If you let me use Father's gun, I'm sure I could shoot some. Cornelius Epp told me they had had some, and the meat tasted very good. He called them prairie chickens."

Mrs. Sperling had carefully guarded her husband's gun and had not allowed even her grown sons to touch it. She was afraid of it, and even though she knew her sons had been trained to use it, they might be careless and someone could be killed. Her husband had enjoyed hunting and had shot various predators to prevent loss to their livestock back in Russia. For a moment she was taken by sadness at her loss, but then she gained control and spoke. "I will think about it. If the job materializes, we will discuss this some more." Then she turned to her daughter, Thelma. "I hope you will work hard for Mrs. Friesha. The money you get will be a big help. Maybe someone will want you to help too, Tina. Rachel and I can get along here with the little ones. Willie and Esther can help with Alvin and Daniel. If we all work together, we will make it, with God's help."

Similar conversations were held in most of the homes. Everyone was hoping the railroad would be built to Henderson. Mr. Kroeker was already planning to build a granary near where the tracks would go. He would buy grain and sell it to the markets in the cities further east. It would be a good business. Mr. Klippenstein was planning to set up a farm supply business. The people who had been in the area several years had been successful, and they would want to buy new equipment to make their work easier. Mr. Pauley was anxious for the railroad to be in operation. It would benefit his business tremendously. Hauling lumber by wagon from York or Sutton was slow work, and it was almost impossible to keep up with the demand. Mr. Ratzloff wanted to set up a general merchandise store, and if the railroad came, it would be possible. He knew the new settlers would soon need fabrics, pots and pans, lamps, and other household items and farm equipment. So the dreams grew. Hopefully, they would come true. If the railroad came they would not be dependent on the Englisha in either York or Sutton.

At the Epp home, the conversation was also hopeful. The younger Hoinz was hoping he could get a job with the railroad. Maybe by spring he would have something to offer little Lena Franzen. He hoped none of the other young men in the community would see how beautiful she was and what a good worker she was. He was sure that she had some feeling for him. *But you never know what is in the minds of young women nowadays,* he thought.

Mrs. Kroeker was true to her word, and at four o'clock she drove up to the soddy with her horse and buggy. Hoinz and Cornelius dashed out of the house eager to help her with the horse. She, however, maintained that she could not stay more than a minute, because she had to get back before dark and the sun was setting so early this time of year. Katharina insisted she come in for a minute. She surely could drink a cup of coffee before she needed to return.

"The coffee is ready to be poured. We even splurged and Maria baked a pastry in case we should have company. I surely miss the old country where we had company almost every Sunday afternoon."

"I guess I can stay long enough for that, if it is ready. It is good to see you and your home. It looks like you are quite comfortable here."

The ladies visited for a few minutes, speaking of their hopes for the railroad and of the family they had left behind in Russia.

Katharina spoke of her daughter Sarah, who had stayed behind in Russia with her husband Peter to care for his aging parents. "I wonder if she is well. Maybe she is with child, and I am not there to help her. They hope to come to this country sometime in the future. I wish they could have come with us, but I don't know if I want her to share the hardships here. They have a comfortable house in Russia."

Mrs. Kroeker replied, "I left two sisters in Russia, so I am lonesome, too. But I think it is good we came here. If the railroad comes through, we will all be much better off. Henry is quite sure it will come."

Maria had tied up her everyday dress, a shawl, and her comb and brush and was ready to leave. With instructions from her mother to work hard, they all shook hands, and then they took their leave. Little Peter and Johann looked like they would break down and cry, but

Maria assured them they would see her next Sunday. Anna would play with them and Sunday would come soon.

"My, this is a fine buggy! And what a good-looking horse. I miss our horses. The oxen are so slow, but they are better at breaking the sod. I should not complain." Maria tried to make polite conversation.

Mrs. Kroeker replied, "We started out with oxen three years ago. Now Mr. Kroeker has rented his land to the Penners. Our house will be ready to live in in another month. I am excited about that. The Penners will live in our soddy until they can build a house of lumber."

Just as the sun set, they arrived at the Kroeker home. Maria was a bit apprehensive of her new duties, but Mrs. Kroeker assured her she would do fine. "I will tell you what to do and how to do it. Don't worry." She showed her the cot near the kitchen stove where she could sleep and keep her things and then asked if she would go get water to fill the stone jar by the door.

Night came, and to save kerosene, everyone went to bed early. In the morning there would be work to do.

Thelma Sperling had a similar experience at the Friesha home. Although there were no children to care for, there was plenty to do. Mrs. Friesha, with a child due to arrive any day, was awkward and uncomfortable, so Thelma started right in. First she brought in twisted grass from the stable end of the house. She noticed that Mr. Friesha had stocked a great supply. They had a cow. That was a surprise. Not many settlers had been able to purchase one.

Mr. Friesha explained, "The Will Jantzens have been here two years, and they have purchased several cows. They are renting this one to us. If and when the railroad comes through, they hope to sell cream and butter to people in York. But now they have more milk than they can use, so they let us have the cow until the railroad comes.

This is a good deal for us. All we have to do is feed her until that time comes. I hope to get work building the railroad and so be able to get our own cow by next summer. It all depends on the railroad."

"My mother keeps telling us the railroad might not come, that we need to trust in God." And then Thelma clapped her hands over her mouth, "I did not mean to be rude," she whispered.

Mr. Friesha assured her there was no offense and that he, too, realized they needed to trust in God for all things.

With all the hard work to be done, the days went by quickly. When Sunday came, the people were all eager to get to church to see if there was any other word from the railroad. The crowd at church was pleased when, after the service, Mr. Kroeker rose and announced that the railroad would be built. Those who wanted a job were to report to the office in York the next day. If they had oxen to use, they would get extra pay.

Maria was eager to see her family again. She would go home with them after the church service and Mrs. Kroeker would call for her again in the afternoon. As they sat down to the noon meal, Father reached out his hand to Maria.

"Did the Kroekers pay you?" he asked.

"Why, yes." Maria replied. "I have it in my pocket."

"Then hand it over. You surely realized that the money belongs to me. Mother and I have had the expense of raising you and bringing you to this country. Until you are of age, you will bring the money home."

Reluctantly Maria left her seat, and reaching into her pocket, she handed the silver dollar to her father. Soberly she returned to her place at the table. Her dreams of new shoes or perhaps a new Sunday dress evaporated. She realized her family had needs, and that she must honor her father and mother. Why had she even thought of spending that dollar on her own dreams?

Cautiously, Hoinz approached his father. "I would like to work for the railroad, if that is agreeable with you. And do you expect me to give my pay to you? I was hoping to earn enough to buy some land for myself."

"You are of age, but if you want to live here, you need to give half of your pay to us. You can use the oxen whenever I don't need them, but the extra pay will come to me. I will need the oxen tomorrow. Just because we are having warm days doesn't mean we won't have a cold winter. I will be going to the Blue River area to see if I can find some wood for fuel when the days grow cold. The knotted hay works fine, but it burns up too fast. We need wood to keep this place warm for the cold days ahead."

Father's word was the law, and Hoinz dared not refute it. He would still earn money for land, but it would take longer to amass what was needed for a land purchase.

Thelma, too, went home with her family. She would walk to the Friesha house later that day. It was only two miles. When she got there, she noticed a strange horse and buggy tied to the post near the door. *Who could that be?* she thought. Upon entering, Mr. Friesha greeted her beaming from ear to ear. "I have a son! Soon I will have help with the farming."

Thelma smiled, "I don't think he will be of much help for some time. But it is good. Is Mrs. Friesha all right?"

Just then the doctor came out of the bedroom. "You have a strong healthy boy. Your wife should stay in bed for a week or so. Then she will be able to resume her work. I am glad you have some help." He gave a few instructions as to the care of the newborn and left, saying he would come by sometime during the week to see how everyone was doing.

Thelma was thrilled at the opportunity to care for the new baby boy and also Mrs. Friesha. She remembered caring for her younger siblings in the past. This was nothing new to her.

The next day at the Epp family home everyone was up early. Father was getting ready to go to the river area to look for firewood. He had intended to take Abraham and Margaret with him, but Mother declared she needed Margaret to help with the washing. Anna, Johann, and Peter begged to go with their father. He relented but gave them strict orders that they would have to work picking up sticks. Mother packed some *Tvaebuck* and cold prairie chicken for their lunch. They would be gone all day.

It was fun for the children to ride in the wagon, and they were excited to know they would be able to help. At the end of the day, they were tired, and Peter and Johann fell asleep on the way home. Father was pleased. The wagon was piled high with wood, many large logs that could be chopped later into burning sized pieces. He would go again the next day and take some of the Sperling children with him. Then they could be secure. They would stay warm through the oncoming winter.

So days and weeks passed, with the weather remaining unusually calm. The work on the railroad progressed, although slowly. Many of the young men in the community worked to prepare the grade. The money they brought home to their families brought encouragement to the households that had risked so much to find freedom to worship as they felt the Bible taught. The money bought sugar, salt, shoes, and clothing for needy people. In most cases it would also bring a little extra for the Christmas celebration which was approaching.

Mothers were looking ahead to this occasion with the hope that they would have a little something to put beside each plate at the breakfast table on that most special of all holidays.

On Sundays they visited with other women and often found ways to exchange various items of clothing that were still wearable but outgrown. Although not new, they would be new to the receiver.

Katharina was given a muslin dress by Mrs. Ratzloff that was sure to fit Maria. She would soak it in some beet juice until it became a beautiful wine color. It would be new to Maria.

Mrs. Sperling managed to find something for each of her children as well. She knew Jake's heart for Elizabeth Fast, and she decided he should have something to give her at Christmas. She wasn't sure that it was wise for him to be interested in a woman with five children. But if that was his desire, she would not stand in his way. She appreciated the hard work he was doing on the railroad so the family could have the things they desperately needed.

At last she decided on a cameo brooch that had belonged to her mother. They had been well-to-do in Russia, and she had several brooches of value, at least one for each of her daughters, and since Elizabeth was a good friend of hers, she thought it not improper to make this possible for Jake. Rings and bracelets were frowned upon by the church, but modest brooches were acceptable, as were pendant necklaces.

Chapter Sixteen

On Sunday before Christmas, Mrs. Sperling asked if Jake would walk with her to see her friend Mrs. Fast. She wished to have a private conversation with Jake, which was impossible in the small dugout with all the other children around. "I would like to take her family a few of the prairie chickens Herman has shot. I think her family would like them. They are tasty, and that would give me an opportunity to contribute something to her family's Christmas dinner. I would like to visit Elizabeth's parents, the Bergens, and get to know all of them better. It is hard to find time to visit. Thelma is home today so she can watch the rest of the family and fix *Faspa* for them."

As they drew near to Elizabeth's parents' house she reached into her pocket and withdrew the brooch. Turning to Jake, she said, "For some time I have suspected that you have an interest in Elizabeth. If that is so, would you like to give her this Christmas present?"

Jake drew a deep breath and said, "I think she is a remarkable woman, and yes, I would like to have her for my wife, but what can I offer her? You need all I can earn for our family."

Mrs. Sperling replied, "Since the sod has been turned on our eighty acres, I think Herman can also work for the railroad. We can manage with his pay and what Thelma brings home. You can use your pay to buy the forty acres near those Elizabeth has purchased. I

139

don't want to deprive you of your future with Elizabeth, if that is the future you want. It is taking on a big responsibility with those five children, even if they are well-behaved. We will see how it works out. Maybe you could ask her to go for a little walk and you will have the opportunity to speak to her privately. I don't suppose you would like to tell of these plans in front of that whole family." She turned and smiled at her oldest son.

"Oh, Mother! Thank you so much for this help! If this works out, I will find the time to come home often and help Herman with the work at home."

They were greeted at the Bergen home by Martha, Albert, and Matilda, who had been playing outside. Albert was riding the stick horse, while the two girls had found some substantial weed stalks. Pretending came easy for them, and they were having a great time. They rushed to take Jake's hand, each of them crowding near him. Finally Martha reached over and took Mrs. Sperling's hand instead, and together they walked to the house.

"We have company!" they shouted as they neared the door. Their mother met them, reminding them to not make so much noise. She welcomed her old friend and son Jake.

"Come in, come in," she said enthusiastically. "It is so good to see you both. Mother and Father will be so happy to see you. I have told them how kind you were to me on the trip, and how you, too, suffered loss on the journey." Then she turned to Jake. Smiling she said, "That poor horse has traveled almost as far as we did coming from Russia. Albert is so pleased with him."

Jake replied, "I should have bought two more, but I didn't know little girls rode horses."

"That was totally unnecessary. They are satisfied with those sticks, and they spend more time playing with their dolls. Albert has a hard time getting them to play with horses. Sometimes he has to play dolls with them just to get them to play horses, but in this nice weather I like to have them play outside. We will be cooped up soon enough when the weather turns cold."

Their plans did work out, and after a short time visiting with the Bergens, Jake asked if Elizabeth would like to show him the land she had purchased from the railroad company, and the two set out in the direction of Elizabeth's property. When Jake mentioned his plans for the future, she stopped, turned to him, and looking at him directly, said, "Do you really want to take on a family of five children? I realize that I cannot be a burden to my family forever, and I did appreciate your friendship on the boat and in New York. I'll admit I had some wild daydreams about you and me, but I never dreamed they would become a reality."

Flustered, Jake had to take a deep breath before he replied, "I am sure this can work out, and by spring we could have a soddy built and could be married, if it isn't too soon after Johann's death."

"I will speak to my parents. Maybe we should wait until fall. It would seem more proper."

"It will be hard for me to wait that long, since you have agreed, but when should we speak to your parents? I would like to be with you when they give their consent. Maybe I can help to persuade them that this would be a good thing."

Elizabeth agreed, and they returned to the house. Catherine Sperling could see immediately that her son's plans had succeeded by the glow on their faces as they entered the house. Elizabeth's parents greeted them warmly. Apparently Catherine had divulged a little of this to the Bergens while they had been out. *Faspa* was ready, and they all gathered around the table. Mr. Bergen gave thanks and then began speaking of the unusually warm weather. Soon the meal was finished, and the children went out to play. Now was the time.

Jake cleared his throat several times until Mr. Bergen at last helped out by asking him what was on his mind. "I hope you are not coming down with a cold. You sound like you might have a sore throat."

"Not at all. But I do have a difficult request, which I hope you will not deny. I have become very interested in your daughter Elizabeth. I know she is of age and free to make her own decision, but we would like your blessing. She has agreed to become my wife. I promise I will provide for her and her children. I will treat them as my own." Jake simply ran out of breath. Never had he made such a long speech about such a difficult subject.

Mr. Bergen spoke again. "My dear young man, you have your mother, brothers, and sisters to care for. How can you possibly take on the responsibility of a wife and five children?"

Jake replied, "Mother and I talked about this on our way over here," and he went on to tell of his prospects.

Mr. Bergen turned to Jake's mother, and she nodded in agreement. Then he turned to his wife, "What do you think of this, Mary?"

Mary nodded in agreement as she saw the hopeful look on her daughter's face, and then spoke. "I think you best not speak of this until fall. It is too soon after Johann's death, but then I would welcome you into the family."

It was time for Mrs. Sperling and Jake to start home if they were to get there before dark. Jake decided to wait until Christmas Eve to give her the brooch. Somehow he would manage to get her alone for a few minutes after the Christmas Eve church service.

On the day before Christmas, Hoinz again needed the oxen. He would go to Sutton to purchase some staples for the rest of the winter. He was sure the mild weather would change, and he did not want his family to be caught unprepared. So Nick Thiezen, Hoinz, and Cornelius, along with Jake and Herman Sperling, walked to the site where they had left off working the day before. It was hard work, and the long walk added to their fatigue, but they were determined to earn that extra cash, both to aid their families and to help them get a start for themselves. Jake was even more motivated now that he had his mother's approval and Elizabeth's consent. He walked so fast the others finally questioned as to his motivation.

"The sooner we get this railroad built, the sooner we will be able to quit work on it. We must get it done before spring work begins." He dared not tell them what his real motivation was. Hoinz, too, seemed more motivated.

Meanwhile, at the Epp household, the family was eagerly awaiting Father's return from Sutton. Would he bring anything special for Christmas? Mother was especially anxious. Dare she hope there might be a letter from their daughter in Russia? She tried not to think about it, but the more she tried not to think about it, the more it ran through her mind.

When Father finally returned, they clamored around him. "Did you bring us something for Christmas?" the younger ones kept asking.

Father answered quietly. "If I did, you will have to wait until tomorrow to find out." But the twinkle which had been absent from their father's eyes for so long seemed to be back. And the clamor subsided as they realized they would have to wait.

Mother cast a questioning eye toward her husband, and he reached into his shirt pocket. Pulling out a wrinkled and slightly torn envelope, he said, "This cannot wait." And he handed the envelope to Mother.

When she saw the envelope she burst into tears, and through her sobs, mumbled as she handed it back. "Here, you open it. I am too shaken to even see the writing."

So Father took out his pocket knife, and after carefully opening the envelope, unfolded the paper and began to read.

"To my dear family in America: We trust that you have arrived safely and have a warm roof over your head. The funeral for Mr. Fast was well attended. We had a very good crop and everyone is doing well. Mr. Regier got kicked in the stomach by one of those fancy horses he bought at such a bargain. It is predicted that he will recover but he was unable to help with the harvest. So the neighbors helped Mrs. Regier and her family. Their son, Karl, has really grown and filled out. He did well in helping. He is working hard on the chores, so they don't need outside help for that. The church is doing well, although we miss those that left us.

"Peter's parents are still with us. They do seem to be getting weaker all along. His mother does not get out of bed some mornings. We may have a surprise for you in the coming spring. We hope to get a letter from you soon, although we know it is expensive to mail, and it takes a long time for letters to travel over the ocean and the rest of the way to us. We pray for you daily, that your health will be good and God will bless you and keep you. Love, Sarah and Peter. P.S. Peter's folks send greetings, as do all the people in the church. Karl Regier asked if we had heard from you. I don't know if he misses Abraham or Maria."

Father looked up to see Mother collapse into the crude rocker he had built out of barrel staves. "Are you all right?" he asked as he walked over to her.

She replied in a shaky voice, "Yes. God be praised they are well. It was just too much for me to get such good news."

As soon as the men came home from their work on the railroad, they ate a hasty supper. The younger children were already washed and dressed in the best they had. The older boys were urged to hurry in their cleanup so they would not be late for the Christmas Eve program at the church. They all had pieces to recite and songs to sing. It wasn't long before they were on their way.

They stopped to pick up Mrs. Sperling and her family. It was a joyful group that was crowded into the large hay wagon. Mrs. Sperling sat on the wagon seat with Father and Mother, while all the children huddled in the wagon bed. On the way, Father started singing, *"Stille Nacht, Heilige Nacht"*[23], and they all joined in. What a merry group it was! As they neared the church, they heard the voices coming from other approaching wagons, and soon the air was filled with Christmas greetings. *"Fröhliche Weihnachten!"* Abraham proudly called out, "Merry Christmas." He was proud that he had learned the English words to the Christmas greeting.

The service went well. The children were excited, and a few forgot their lines, but all in all, it was a magnificent service.

After the service, the young people crowded into the Kroekers' wagon to go caroling. This is what they had done traditionally in Russia, and they were determined to continue the custom in the new country.

---

[23] "Silent Night, Holy Night"

Margaret was excited to be allowed to go with the young people. This was the first time she was considered old enough to go. She found herself sitting between Maria and Frank Penner, which pleased her greatly. Maria was uncomfortable with Ben Goosen beside her, while Hoinz had managed to locate himself next to little Lena Franzen. This occasion was one time when the young people could socialize, and they were determined to make the best of it. Life demanded long, hard hours of work, so whenever there was time for relaxing and pleasure, they took advantage of it. The night had turned cold, and that gave the young men an excuse to cuddle closer to their chosen lady friends.

Jake had made arrangements to borrow a buggy from the pastor, so he took Elizabeth to her home. Elizabeth's parents, the Bergens, had agreed to take the children.

It was well past midnight before every one returned to his own home. Jake was the last at the Sperling household because he had returned the buggy to the pastor and then walked home.

The three Epp girls were too excited to sleep. Katie was the first to whisper. "How did you like to sit so close to that Goosen boy?" she whispered to Maria.

"I was uncomfortable. I hope he doesn't get the idea I like him, because I don't. There wasn't a single young man I was interested in. But I think Margaret is getting a little sweet on Frankie Penner."

Embarrassed, Margaret denied it, but secretly she did think he was pretty nice. She spoke up to Maria, "I think Ben is a good man. Why did you ignore him the way you did? Are you still thinking about Karl Regier in Russia? You will never see him again."

Maria did not reply, and soon the tired girls fell asleep.

146

Christmas morning came too soon for the older children, but the little ones were up early to see what *Sinterclaus* [24] had brought. Shrieks of joy filled the house as they found gifts next to their plates. Anna hugged the rag doll her mother had managed to make out of scraps she had brought from Russia. Johann looked with dismay at the sled Father had made with scrap lumber left from building the ceiling and roof of the soddy.

He exclaimed, "What good is a sled? There is no snow in Nebraska."

Father lifted him up in his strong arms and assured him there would be plenty of snow before too long. And Johann was satisfied.

Father called up to the loft, "Time to get up! There is work to do."

As the older children, with Mr. Thiezen, descended the ladder from the attic, they were surprised to see gifts for each of them at their plates as well. There were two silver dollars each for Katie, Hoinz, and Cornelius. Maria was delighted with her wine-colored dress and excited when she found a silver dollar in the pocket. Father had been generous. He thanked the older children for the hard work they had done over the year and promised that their contribution to the family income would help the family to survive until they could raise a crop the following summer.

Now it did not matter that they had been out late. Work was work, and it had to be done. The Franzen family was coming for dinner, and preparations had to be made. Soon Katie was busy making a *Plautz* with the dough Mother had reserved from the *Tvaebuck* that was rising near the Russian stove Father had built soon after the soddy had been finished.

---

[24] Santa Claus

Mr. Thiezen, with Hoinz and Cornelius, had gone hunting. Perhaps they would find some prairie chickens to add to the holiday feast.

When noon came, they gathered around the family table. Mr. and Mrs. Franzen, with their grown sons, John, Isaac, and Thomas, Nick Thiezen, Mother and Father, Hoinz, and Cornelius found places around the family table, which was spread with platters of roast goose that Abraham had shot the day before as well as the prairie chickens shot that morning. Although they had no potatoes, there were baked beans seasoned with a bit of salted pork, and *Kielkes*[25]. Father asked Mr. Franzen to ask the blessing, which he did, thanking God again for their safe arrival in this good country, where they were free to worship without interference from the government. He thanked Him for health and the friendship of the Epps, and above all for the gift of eternal life through the birth, death, and resurrection of the Son of God. He then asked God to bless the food to their bodies and ended with a loud AMEN.

Katie, Maria, and Margaret were busy serving the food, making sure everything was hot as it was passed around. After the *Plautz* and coffee had been served, they quickly washed the enameled plates and tin forks, knives, and spoons so the rest could eat. The pots and pans could be done later. The children were called in from outdoors, where they had been riding their stick horses, and soon everyone was fed.

Mr. Franzen had brought his violin. Nick got out his harmonica, and soon the whole house rang with the sound of music.

---

[25] home-made noodles

Later that night, Father took out the family Bible and reread the Christmas story. After the family prayers, they all agreed it had been a blessed Christmas.

The second day of Christmas was celebrated much the same as the first, with the exception that there were no gifts, and the Epp family was invited to the Kroekers' house. Here they were all thrilled to see a Christmas carousel that Mr. Kroeker had built. The older children remembered the one they had seen at their grandparents' house in Russia. It brought back memories of their old home and a bit of sadness, which was soon erased as Mr. Kroeker lit the candles on the outside frame. As the heat from the candles rose, the warm air caught the cardboard fins at the top of the pyramid, and the inner structure began to revolve. The three circular shelves of the inner structure held tiny paper figurines. The top shelf held four tiny angels. The middle one held Mary, Joseph, and the baby Jesus in a little paper manger. The lower one held the three wise men and the shepherds, with a few little *papier-mâché* sheep. It was like magic to the younger children, and Father resolved to build one for his family the next year. When the day ended, they went home tired but happy. It had been a lovely Christmas, and things looked promising for the New Year.

Chapter Seventeen

On New Year's Eve, people gathered for a Watch Night Service. Since this service was scheduled to last until midnight, many of the mothers had decided to stay home with younger children. The teenagers and those in their early twenties thought it was exciting to be able to stay up this late. There was much singing and a time for individuals to speak about blessings of the year 1874 and also their hopes for 1875. The congregation was hopeful for the future. They would be free to go about their business without Mr. Todtleben to come around demanding payment in exchange for exemption from military service.

New Year's Day was spent relaxing for all but Mother and the older girls. They were busy making *Neeyoish Kuka*[26]. This, along with the *Paepa Naeta*[27] left from Christmas would be their *Faspa* today.

Early in the afternoon, clouds began to gather, and those who had been visiting started for home. The host family sent *Paepa Naeta* and *Neeyoish Kuka* with the departing guests.

Father stepped out of the soddy periodically to check the skies. He was sure this would prove to be a major storm. Late in the afternoon

---

[26] *Neujahrskekse*, New Year's Cookies; small spoonfuls of yeast dough with raisins, deep fried to a golden crisp and rolled in sugar

[27] *Pfeffernüsse*, or peppernuts: small spicy cookies

the wind began to blow, and before dark it began to snow. When morning came, it was still snowing, and the wind was blowing hard. How thankful they were to have such a warm home! The soddy was much warmer than the houses that had been so hastily constructed of expensive lumber. There would be no working on the railroad for a few days. But the knotted grass and the wood he had hauled from the Blue River area would keep them comfortable. The days were spent playing "Hide the Thimble," "I Spy," and other games they remembered playing through stormy days in Russia. They were happy for the storm, for it would help prepare the turned sod into workable soil for the spring planting.

After three days the storm subsided, but the air turned very cold. Father and Hoinz put on the warm clothing and sheepskin coats brought from Russia and ventured out to see what damage the storm might have done to the soddy's roof. After it was checked out, they decided to walk over to Mrs. Sperling's to make sure she had survived the storm as well. Mrs. Sperling was happy to see them and immediately put coffee on the stove. She was especially grateful for the sizeable stack of wood that Mr. Epp had brought from the river. The rest of the day the men spent working in the barn end of the soddy. It was fairly warm there, with the body heat from the oxen and the activity they were engaged in. When they reentered the house in time for supper, they announced that they would be able to go to church next Sunday, for they had just made sled runners out of barrel staves. Instead of wheels, the wagon now had runners.

Little Johann was clamoring to go outside and try his new sled. So although it was very cold, his brother Hoinz bundled him up and gave him a ride around the area of the soddy. He promised that on

Monday they would take the sled to a nearby hillside and slide, if he promised to let his sisters have a ride or two.

At church the horses with buggies were lined up in a row on the south side of the building. Most of the horses had blankets to keep them warm during the church service. The oxen were tough, so they were tethered wherever it was convenient.

It was good to see the many friends and neighbors again after the storm, although there was disconcerting news that two of the Quiring boys had been out hunting the day of the storm and had not come back. The family hoped they had found shelter with some other settlers. When they did not appear with anyone at church, the family's alarm grew, and the men immediately organized a search party. Sadly, they reported back that no trace of the two boys could be found. They would look again the next day. Perhaps they had found shelter under a creek bank somewhere.

The boys were not found until the first of February, when much of the snow had melted. They had frozen to death just fifty feet from their home. The community grieved together as they came to the first funeral in the new country. The men dug the graves with pick and shovel through the frozen ground, and the bodies were laid to rest near the church building. There were other funerals that winter: old Mr. Peters died of consumption; six-year-old Minnie Schierling got sick with a fever and died a few days later.

The people of the community grieved together, and yet their faith in the hereafter grew stronger after each tragedy. They often sang Mrs. Sperling's favorite song, "Oh, They Tell of a Home Far Beyond the Skies."

There were other snowstorms, but the settlers were extra cautious now. If clouds appeared, they made sure that everyone found shelter long before the storm hit.

Toward the last of February, Father suggested they try the sod-buster plow on Nick Thiezen's home site. He thought that the warm weather might have softened the earth enough for the oxen to turn it up. It worked well, and so the men were busy again from early morning to late evening, building a home for Mr. Thiezen. They did not go home for the noon meal, since that would have taken too much time from their work. Instead, they sent Abraham to get whatever had been cooked. Mr. Thiezen had decided to build his home exactly like that of the Epps, but a bit smaller. The clay subsoil floor had proven to be more satisfactory than floors on which the black soil had been left in place. The indentation, too, made it warmer. As soon as the walls were high enough, he would borrow Mr. Epp's wagon and go to Sutton to buy lumber to finish the ceiling and the roof. The attic area would be a good place to store bags of grain the next winter. The work went well, and after a few days, it was determined that, with one more day's labor, the walls would be up. They were working so diligently that they didn't notice the time until they saw Katie coming toward them carrying the lunch basket. Nick went to greet her and to help her carry the sizeable basket.

He spoke. "We were so busy working we forgot it was noon. Here. Let me carry that. What have you fixed for us today?" He knew full well it would be the same rye bread with brown lard and *Plautz* or maybe *Snetya*.[28] "I sure do appreciate the cooking you have done to make this house possible for me."

---

[28] A pastry similar to *Plautz*, but folded into triangles

Katie replied, "For a brother, it is not work. How near finished are you? It will seem strange not having you at our house. We have become used to you, and you seem like a member of the family."

Nick looked the other way, and answered so quietly she could barely hear. "I want to be a member of the family, but not a brother."

What could he possibly mean by that? Katie thought. But she didn't say anything. Then they reached the place where the others were working, so no more was said.

After the men had eaten and were resting on the grass for a few minutes, Nick asked Katie if she would like to see the inside of what had been built. She agreed, and so the two walked over to the soddy and through the door opening. Nick showed her where he planned to place the meager furniture that was stored in the loft at the Epp house above the oxen. He explained how he would build a Russian stove just like Mr. Epp had built, with brick he hoped to get in Sutton the next day. Suddenly he was overcome and his shoulders shook with a dry sob.

Brokenly he said, "I think my Anna would have been pleased with it."

In sympathy, Katie put her hand on his shoulder and said softly, "I'm sure she would have been. I know it has been hard for you to go on without her. She was a wonderful woman. I miss her too! She was a good friend."

Quite suddenly she found Nick's arms around her and his head on her shoulder. "I miss her so! And I had such high hopes for us. That tiny little boy was so beautiful. Why did God have to take them from me?"

Katie was totally caught by surprise. Her only wish was to comfort this poor man that had suffered such great loss.

After just a minute or two, Nick composed himself and apologized. "I don't know what came over me. But Katie, it did feel awfully good to hold you in my arms. I may want to do it again some time. Please don't think me rash, but don't think of me as a brother either. I think of you often, but not as a sister."

They heard the other men approaching. It was time to get back to work if the walls were to be finished that day.

The next day Nick got ready to go to Sutton. He had planned to go alone, but at the last minute, Father had decided to go with him. They were gone until late afternoon. The family saw Nick coming back with the wagon loaded with lumber, but Father was not with him. However, Nick had a cow tied to the back of the wagon.

"Did you trade my husband for a cow?" Katharina asked with a smile.

"Not really! This cow needed a new home, so we all chipped in, and now we can all have milk to drink. Your husband will be here pretty soon. He had some other business to tend to. When I left him, he was trying to drive a hard bargain with a Mr. Phelps." And then, looking back, he said, "I think I see him coming now."

Katharina looked in the direction Nick pointed and saw two horses approaching with what seemed like a double buggy behind him.

"What on earth?!" she gasped. "How could he have enough money to buy that?"

Nick grinned as he replied, "Well, Mr. Phelps was mighty eager to get a new team that was livelier, and by selling the cow and the team and carriage, he could get a fancier rig."

There was such excitement over the purchases that supper was forgotten for some time. But at last order was restored. The horses were safely tethered beside the oxen and the carriage at the other end of the barn.

The family gathered around the supper table. Thanks were given, and everyone was busy eating when Father suddenly got up. "Goodness! We forgot that that cow has to be milked. Who volunteers for the job?"

Mother was the first to offer, but Katie said, "Mother is too old. I will do the honors."

She soon returned to the house with a bucket of milk, and all had a drink. Oh, how good it was! And the next day they would have cream with their coffee. The *Tvaebuck* would taste so much better with milk in the dough. Things were looking up.

It wasn't until she had gone to bed that Katie again thought of the incident at Nick's soddy. What should she make of it? Was it just a reflex action on his part? But what about the comment about being a part of the family but not a brother? Over and over these thoughts raced through her mind until she heard Father call, "Time to get up!" She didn't realize she had gone to sleep.

With the first of March came warm weather, and the farmers became eager to get to work planting their crops. Oats and rye seeds were soon scattered over the overturned sod. Garden plots were prepared, and patiently people waited for the time to plant potatoes, onions, turnips, beans, rutabaga, and other vegetable seeds they had brought from the homeland. They eagerly awaited the arrival of fresh vegetables to add to their monotonous diet.

Those who had weathered several years in the new country showed the newcomers what native plants could be eaten. Sheep sorrel was picked and eaten by the children; it had a sour taste, but they didn't mind. Mother made *Mos*[29] with it as well. It was something different. The *Kaiskie Kruit*[30] was also enjoyed, even though it had very little taste. The children ate it for the sheer novelty.

---

[29] a soup made by cooking the weed with white sauce
[30] a round-leafed weed with a tiny round seed encased in a green husk

Chapter Eighteen

April continued warm. Spring wheat, barley, rye, and oats had been planted. Eagerly the farmers checked their fields to see what was sprouting, and before long, the countryside had a light green haze to it. Oh, how good it was to see that! The early plantings in the gardens were beginning to grow. Mother was delighted to see the tiny green leaves of the *Paipa Kraut*[31] she had planted. How she longed to have some of this savory weed to add to her soups. The soup just didn't taste the same without it. Mother watched with patience the site where she had planted the rhubarb root that Mrs. Kroeker had given her. When she saw the ground bulge and the evidence of growth, she gave out a shout like a teenager, bringing the rest of the family running. Never had they heard this from their normally quiet mother. The family rejoiced with her.

And then came the dreaded news: The grasshoppers that had plagued the earlier settlers the year before had laid eggs in the soil. With this warm weather, they were hatching. The land was simply crawling with little green insects. Soon they would start eating, and all the hard work of the settlers would be for naught, plus the precious seed would be gone. What were they to do?

---

[31] *Pfefferkraut:* pepperweed

Their only resource was prayer, and how they prayed that God would remove this plague from them. Were they to suffer all the plagues of Egypt before they would harvest a crop in this new land? Where was the God who had directed them to this land?

Pastor Unruh called a special prayer meeting, and it was well attended. The fathers with families were the most downhearted. How could they survive another year without a crop? Their hunting had brought sufficient meat to their tables, but without flour there would be no bread. Could they live on meat alone?

Hoinz was remorseful. He was glad they had bought the cow, but he should not have bought the team of horses and that carriage. After all, only the oxen were needed. Perhaps he could sell the carriage. He really would like to keep the horses. They would make future plowing much faster and easier. But in these hard times, who would buy the horses or the carriage?

A sense of gloom permeated the entire community. But then, three days after the special prayer meeting, a dark cloud arose in the western sky. Many people prayed it would rain enough to drown every grasshopper in the state. It did rain, and the weather turned considerably cooler for about a week. After the sun came out again, the farmers found that the green grasshoppers were dead. Later, they learned that in cool wet weather, the young grasshoppers did not eat, thus preventing their bodies from maturing to the adult stage.

Most of the settlers attributed this miracle to an act of God. The church was filled with worshipers on Sunday, and additional prayers of praise and thanksgiving were uttered.

After a few days of sunshine, the farmers noted another benefit from the wet spell. Where the tiny grain seed had sprouted, the plant had stooled out. There were now five little stalks coming where there had been only one.

Hoinz expressed it for all the people in his prayer at the breakfast table a week later. "Our most gracious Lord, forgive us for doubting; forgive our unbelief. We are a sinful people, but have mercy on us. Give us the faith of a mustard seed. Help us to rely on You for all our needs. Make us to walk in Your path. Forgive us for grumbling and complaining, and make us to be content with what we have. You have promised to never leave us nor forsake us. Help us to remember that, and to trust in Your Son, who so willingly died for our redemption. AMEN."

That evening, as the sun was setting, Father asked Mother to step outside for a minute. He had something he wanted to show her. First he showed her the tiny green buds on a row of sticks he had stuck in the ground along the wagon path. Then he took her to the side of the soddy and pointed to some smaller twigs sticking out of the ground nearby. "See the shape of those leaves? Can you tell me what they are?"

Tears of joy glistened in Mother's eyes. "Are those lilac bushes?"

"They are the offspring of your bush in Russia. I did not tell you about them because I was afraid they would not grow. But see? There they are. God has blessed us beyond our dreams. They probably won't have blooms for several years, but it is a start."

Tears of joy streamed down her cheeks as she reached for her husband's hand, but all she could manage to say was a simple "Thank you!" as, hand in hand, they walked back to the house.

Days and weeks passed. The railroad was inching closer to the town of Henderson, but the work was slow, since most of the former workers were now engrossed in farming. Whenever there was a day that the farm did not demand attention, the young men would walk to the construction site to offer help. That dollar a day would help keep the proverbial wolf from the door, and idleness was a tool of the Devil.

Nick Thiezen had moved into his newly built soddy. Although Katie saw very little of him, Father, Hoinz, Cornelius, and Abraham often spoke to him if they happened to be working near his place. Abraham usually had the job of taking him a quart of milk after the cow had been milked in the evening.

Nick Thiezen received many invitations for Sunday dinners and accepted most of them. These invitations usually came from families who had eligible daughters. More than one mother in the community had hopes of having the industrious Mr. Thiezen for a son-in-law. If the invitation proved to be too obvious, Nick politely declined. The hostess usually sent *Plautz, Tvaebuck*, and other baked goods home with him, sometimes with the comment that her daughter had done the baking.

Mother usually sent *Tvaebuck* with Abraham when he delivered the milk on Saturdays. He reported back that Nick was getting along fairly well. He had learned to cook the prairie chickens as well as rabbits. With the baked goods given to him, he was getting along. Katie wondered if he ever thought about the comments he had made to her that day inside his unfinished soddy. She told herself to forget it, but of course the more she tried to forget, the more it came to mind. She must fill her mind with other things. With the coming of harvest, that was easier to do.

As Independence Day drew near, Pastor Unruh urged the congregation to cease their harvesting and come to worship and give thanks for the bountiful grain crop and for the freedoms of this great country. In all this time, there had been no government official call on them for revenue.

It was also rumored that the first train would arrive in Henderson that day. There would be a great celebration in the little village. Main Street was looking prosperous. It now boasted a hotel, lumberyard, blacksmith shop, livery barn, general merchandise store, and grain company. The future looked promising. And although the Mennonites normally frowned on excessive celebrating, Pastor Unruh thought it fitting that they celebrate, of course giving praise and glory to God, who had made it all possible.

There had been funerals: The plot where the two Quiring boys had been laid to rest now held twenty graves. This had to be accepted. The settlers were familiar with disease, accidents, and old age. They looked toward those markers each Sunday with sadness but acceptance, nonetheless.

There had been weddings, too. Although not the celebrations that they had enjoyed in Russia, the marriages usually took place after the morning church service on Sunday. Just a simple procedure of repeating the traditional vows was all that was really necessary. It was true that the unions were simply a necessity. A widow needed the help of a widower who was also in need. And although the marriages came about with little courtship or romance, they endured. The promises were made and kept. True love and devotion often grew later. Sometimes love did not develop; bitterness and resentment took root, but nevertheless, the vows were kept.

The Independence Day celebration was observed with a picnic on the shady side of the church building. The settlers had just finished the meal and were lounging about on the grass, and the babies had been nursed and were sleeping on the mothers' shoulders, when they heard the lonesome sound of the whistle of the steam engine. Not caring if the babies awakened, the mothers quickly handed them over to the fathers. Younger children were told to hang onto the hands of older children, and *en masse* the congregation moved toward the site where the station house foundation had been laid. The train was really coming. Excitement rang high throughout the crowd.

The crowd cheered as the train crept closer and closer. Again the whistle blew, and the crowd covered their ears. The babies cried, while slightly older children hung on more tightly to the older siblings, who had been instructed to make sure to hold their hands. Some of the teenage boys dared each other to step closer to the tracks, but when the engineer pulled the lever that shot out a burst of steam, even the bravest jumped back in fear.

At last it came to a full stop, and the engineer climbed to the ground. He shook hands with some of the community leaders and then was offered coffee and pastries from the welcome table nearby. The conductor walked up to the crowd, shook hands, and, after having some refreshments, invited some of the young men to come take a look at the caboose. They were amazed at the comforts it offered. There was a heating stove, a cot, and a table next to the cot.

"You could live comfortably in this," one of the young men commented.

Abraham Epp replied, "I intend to do that. When I come of age, I want to get a job on the railroad. Just think of sitting in that car all day, just making sure the train cars get left at the proper siding. It would sure beat sod busting all day."

The next day it was back to the hard work of the farms. Everyone was hopeful for a good harvest, and it turned out to be just that. Mr. Abe Braun announced after church one Sunday that his mill on the

Blue River just south of town was up and operating. He welcomed the farmers to bring a wagon load of wheat. He would grind it into the finest flour they had seen since leaving Russia.

Even while the women were busy cooking for the harvesters, they managed to tend their gardens. The children were busy tending the cow and weeding the garden. Wild plum bushes had been found in various places along creek banks and along the river. Usually one adult sister and the younger children would walk a mile or two to such a location and pick all day, stopping only to eat a brown lard and rye bread sandwich at noon. They ate the sweet wild plums to their hearts' content and later realized their stomachs were not used to this delicacy. The consequences followed, but there was no serious illness related to it – just a few days of discomfort. Plums were dried, and jam was made, even if sugar was expensive. Next winter there would be plum jam along with the brown lard on their bread.

There was talk in the community of starting a school for children between the ages of six and twelve. Soon work was started on a building for this, and then it was decided that another building should be built for the older children as well. They would be free to attend after the harvesting was done. There was some discussion about whether this should be available to both girls and boys. The argument got quite heated at times between those who favored the education and those who were opposed to it. Those who opposed it stated firmly that all a girl needed to know she could learn from her mother. What did a girl need to know other than cooking, sewing and keeping house?

However, pro-education won out, and girls were welcomed to the school. Many, however, did not take advantage of the opportunity.

Finally the day came for the first year anniversary of their arrival in the state of Nebraska. This called for special recognition. There would be a special church service with a picnic afterward. Everyone was excited! The year had been difficult, dotted with sadness and tragedy, but they had survived. They had harvested grain and garden produce to last them through the winter. Every farmstead had a mound of dirt near the house. As they had done in Russia, they had excavated an area, covered the bottom with straw, and stored cabbages, turnips, carrots, potatoes, and other garden produce there. Then it had been covered with more straw and lastly dirt. This would preserve the food at least until the first of the year. With a cow in the stable, they were assured that they could feast like kings from now on. They had managed to sell enough grain to make reasonable improvements to their living conditions. The precious red winter seed wheat they had brought from Russia was now planted. During the long winter past, some had been tempted to use it for white bread but had resisted. Next year would be easier.

Katie was too old to go to school. She could read and do the four basics of math, but more importantly, she could bake bread and other pastries. She knew how to make *Mus* and *Kielkes*. She had proven her ability with a needle and thread. Mother was proud of the fine seams she made as she patched clothing for the members of the family. On one particular day, as she sat near the bit of light that came through the window, she looked up to see a horse and buggy come driving toward the house. Who could this be on a weekday? The younger children were in school; the men were out working. Margaret, Anna, and Johann were in school, and Mother was nodding off in her rocking chair. Placing her sewing carefully on the table, she stepped over to the door to check.

As she opened the door she was greatly surprised. It was their neighbor, Nick Thiezen. What could he possibly want? And when did he get that beautiful horse and buggy? Quickly she reached up to smooth her hair and make sure none of the pins that held the braid around her head showed. She gave a quick glance at her apron to make sure it did not have food spilled on it. "Why, hello, neighbor!" she called out. "What brings you out in the middle of the day?"

"It is such a lovely day and my work seems to be caught up, so I thought I'd just take a ride. I wondered if you might be able to join me. This horse, you see, needs some exercise," he answered. The horse was impatiently prancing around, eager to go trotting down the road.

"Just a minute, I'll check with Mother. I have *Tvaebuck* dough rising, but maybe Mother can take care of it."

Mother agreed, and Katie was gallantly helped up to the seat in the buggy. "When did you get this fancy rig?" she asked hesitantly.

Nick replied, "I had more oats than I had room to store in my attic, so I took it to Henderson. I couldn't sell it, but Mr. Mireau at the livery stable had a team and buggy that he was willing to trade, so we made a deal. Do you like it?"

"Yes, it is very nice!" Katie didn't think it should make any difference whether she liked it or not, but she was glad he valued her opinion. "He sure is frisky. What is her name?"

"His name is Harry!" and Nick smiled he corrected her. "His teammate is named Nell. Nell is a dapple gray. Harry needs to pull a plow for awhile to get rid of some of his energy. I am going to see if anyone around here needs some plowing done. My ground is all ready for spring planting." With that he picked up the reins and spoke to the horse. "Giddap!" and off they went. He steered the eager horse toward his place, and when they got close, the horse shook his head gaily and whinnied to his mate. She replied, and they pulled up to his house.

"I just wanted you to see how my house looks now that it is finished. It is not fancy, but it is comfortable." He pulled the reins tight and dismounted, walking around to help her down. Then, tying the horse to a post near the stable, he came around to help her down. As she took the long step to the ground, he held her close for a second, or was that her imagination?

Together they walked to the door of the soddy and entered. The place was immaculate. The hard packed clay floor almost shone in the dim light. She could see the clumsy efforts of a man trying to make the place look good. She noticed some of Anna's things that she remembered from having visited their home in Russia. She realized suddenly that it had already been over a year since she had seen Anna, and a moment of sadness filled her heart.

She turned to Nick and spoke. "I think it looks very nice. I see Anna's things, and it makes me miss her."

"I miss her more than I can explain, but she is gone. When I first unpacked her things, I didn't think I could bear to look at them, but I have overcome that. It has been over a year now, and I would like to look to the future. Do you remember last spring when I spoke of being a member of your family but not a brother? I still wish that, and if Anna could speak to me, I think she would say, 'Katharina Epp is the young woman that should take my place in your heart.' I am asking you, Katie, if you would be willing to consider that."

"I wondered about that comment last spring. There are many young women in the community that would love to take Anna's place. Are you sure I could restore joy to your heart?"

"Definitely. I don't expect you to be Anna. She was one-of-a-kind, and I loved her dearly. I know I could grow to love you as well, dear Katie. If you agree, I will speak to your father. You will make me very happy if you say yes." And he looked imploringly into her eyes.

Shyly, she looked up into his dark blue eyes, and then lowering hers, whispered, "Yes. I will do my best to always make you happy. Anna was my dear friend, and her memory will continue in my heart, but I am ready to give you my love."

At this Nick gave out a whoop that startled the horses, and Nick and Katie could hear them stamping around beyond the wall. Then Nick took Katie in his arms, and, whirling her around, said, "Now my house will become a home."

Arm in arm they returned to the buggy and started back for the Epp homestead.

Mother looked up from where she was taking the *Tvaebuck* out of the Russian oven and smiled. She saw the glow on Katie's face and surmised what had taken place. She feared she was losing a daughter but gaining a fine son-in-law. She was pleased. First Sarah and now Katie, and no doubt Hoinz would soon announce he was leaving the nest. *Well, that is the way it is*, she thought. *At least they will live nearby. We will see each other often.*

Meanwhile, Nick had sought out Mr. Epp and broached the subject. Mr. Epp was in agreement. He commented, "I know of no one in the community that I would rather give my daughter to. God bless you and fill your home with joy and gladness."

Chapter Nineteen

Plans for the wedding were made immediately. It would be held at the church with a reception including *Faspa*. For convenience sake, the reception would be at Pastor Unruh's house. It was close to the church and would eliminate the necessity of traveling into the country and then back home in time to do the evening chores. The Epps would furnish the *Tvaebuck* and the sausages they had made after butchering. The coffee would have to be made from the newly harvested barley. Although it didn't taste like the coffee they had enjoyed in Russia, it was an acceptable substitute. Mrs. Sperling and a few others offered to help bake the *Tvaebuck*, since baking such a large quantity would take too long in one of the small Russian ovens. They would also serve *Plautz* with the dried prunes they had preserved. There was an air of excitement in the community. This would be a real wedding celebration like the ones they had enjoyed in Russia.

Katharina dug into the chest she had brought from Russia and brought out her own wedding dress. With a tuck here and there and a hem taken out, it would fit her daughter Katie. Hoinz took Katharina and Katie to Henderson to see if they could find something with which to trim the dress to bring it up to the present style. The mercantile shop had some satin ribbon that would match the material perfectly, and mother and daughter worked late to make little rosettes with the satin. They stitched two rows of satin near the hem and positioned the rosettes at a point in the waist. The dress looked like new. It had already served two brides, and Katie would be the third. How they wished Sarah and Peter could be there for the occasion!

The banns were announced and the carefully worded invitation was sent from house to house in the order of the names were listed on the envelope.

Many of the invited guests came to the bride's house the evening before the wedding. They brought simple gifts and best wishes. No gifts were needed for setting up house, since Nick had all of Anna's household goods. The young people enjoyed this evening of visiting, and because the house was so crowded, they gathered outside for their merry-making. They played a few games, such as "Prisoner's Base," "Too Late for Supper" and then "Last Couple Out." The young men manipulated the games until they were paired off with their sweethearts. Soon various couples left the game to stroll down the wagon path leading to the creek road. The moon added to the evening's pleasure, and more than one betrothal was made, with, of course, the approval of the bride-to-be's father, to be obtained in the near future. The young people were quite unaware that their parents had done a little manipulating and maneuvering to make sure their offspring would pair up with suitable mates.

The younger Hoinz was walking with Lena. As they walked along, he reached for her hand, and, holding it firmly, he spoke of his plans for the future. She listened enthusiastically, and finally he blurted out the words. "I want you to be a part of that future."

She replied, "Oh, Hoinz! I was hoping you would ask me ever since we left Russia."

At hearing these words, Hoinz took her into his arms, and, holding her close, he whispered, "We must get married before the spring work starts. I will speak to your father. Maybe by the middle of January we could be married. I will see if I can find some land to buy or rent, and we can build our house by spring."

Similar conversations were held as the various couples strolled in the moonlight. This great country held great opportunities, and though they realized the hardships that they would no doubt have to endure, they were filled with the enthusiasm of youth and the prospect of a successful future.

A few of the young people found themselves without a partner, so the girls gathered in one group and the men in another. Frequent glances were made across the separation.

The girls were about to return to the house when Frank Penner stopped Maria. Since she had ignored Ben Goosen's advances on Christmas Eve, he hoped he might gain her interest. After all, Margaret was a bit too young for him. He would rather court Maria. She had more spunk and seemed more interesting than Margaret. "Don't you want to walk to the creek with me?" he asked as he attempted to take her arm.

She turned in disgust and said, "No, not really," and hurried to the house with the other girls.

Margaret walked close to her and said quietly, "Why did you turn Frankie down? He is a good man and he has some land and a team of horses. Why don't you like him?"

She replied, "I know he is a good, successful man, but I just don't like his arrogance."

Just then the door of the soddy opened, and everyone realized it was time to go home. Tomorrow would be a great day.

The wedding day dawned bright and sunny, and, although it was cold, a crowd gathered at the church early. Those living far from the church had brought their lunch, which they ate on the sunny side of the church.

As the congregation sang, "*Gott ist die Liebe*,[32]" Katie and Nick walked down the middle aisle of the church. There were *oohs* and *aahs* from the ladies in the congregation when they saw the bride in her wedding dress. The younger women and those recently betrothed pictured themselves walking down the aisle. The older women dabbed at their eyes as they thought of the high hopes they had had as brides and of the hardships of reality that the young couple would soon face. Yet each also had fond memories of that special day when she had been the bride. The ceremony was much like the one Sarah and Peter had experienced four years before. Another song by the congregation and the service was dismissed. They would gather at the parsonage for *Faspa* and a short visit before it would be time to go home to do chores.

Nick helped his new bride into the buggy, wrapped the robe snuggly around her, and then, much to her embarrassment, reached over and gently kissed her on the lips. "My dear," he whispered, "at last you are my wife. I will care for you always. Now my house will be a home. I hope I will make you happy. I have looked forward to this day all summer." He climbed into the other side of the buggy, and they drove off to the sound of well-wishes from the congregation.

When they reached his home he again tightened the reins, jumped down, and helped Katie step down from the buggy. They walked to the door where, much to Katie's surprise, he picked her up, carried

---

[32] "God Is Love"

her into the house, and dumped her into the bed. "I must take care of the horses and milk the cow. Then I will be back."

He had lit the lamp, and as he left she got up and looked around. She would make a few changes here and there, but for the most part, the house looked comfortable.

When Nick returned, she asked, "Would you like something to eat?"

Nick replied, "Just let me feast my eyes on you. There is some bread and some *Plautz* your mom sent over, but I am not hungry. I will set this milk over here, and maybe you could skim the cream in the morning. It sure is good to have cream with my coffee."

Katie hesitated. She had never undressed before a man before. But Nick reassured her, "Don't be afraid, my dear. It is the right thing to do."

So she slipped off her mother's wedding dress, only to have it caught on the combs in her hair. Nick rushed over to help her, and then, holding her gently, he continued to help her out of her clothes.

It was cold in the soddy, and quickly she slipped her new night-gown over her head and crept into their bed. *Is this nervousness what my mother and sister Sarah experienced on their first night with a man?* she thought.

She was happy to have Nick's warm body come close to her, and with the lamp blown out, she cuddled even closer. This was God's plan for marriage, and she yielded to her husband's caresses.

When morning came, Katie awoke with a start. It took her a minute to recognize her surroundings, and then she jumped out of bed. Nick was gone, undoubtedly to milk the cow. She should be getting breakfast for him. He had started a fire, and the house was warming up. She noticed he had an adequate supply of the twisted grass stacked nearby as well as a few small logs to keep the fire burning. First she would skim the milk so it would be ready for the barley brew they called coffee. Then she added a few twists of grass to the stove to make the coffee. She rummaged around to find what she needed, and by the time Nick came in, she had the table set with Anna's tin plates and cups for their first breakfast together.

After her husband read a portion of scripture and prayed a prayer of thanksgiving for health and safety and the joy of his new wife, they ate.

Katie spoke. "Thank you for having the house warmed and for the supply of twisted grass and wood, but from now, on I can tend to those matters. I can milk the cow as well."

To this Nick replied, "It gives me pleasure to do this for you, my dear. When spring work begins, you can take over, but until then, there is no reason why I should not help."

In silence they ate, each deep in thought. At last Katie spoke. "It is so quiet here. At our house it was always a noisy tumult with everyone wanting to say something or be heard. There were often arguments about who could have the last piece of bread or who was crowding. Father often threatened to use his razor strap to diminish the noise."

Nick grinned, "If you think this is quiet, you should have experienced the quiet when I first came to live here, after spending those months at your house. It was really kind of your parents to invite me, especially since their family is so large already. I am glad they did, for it gave me the opportunity to know you better and to realize that, with you, my life would be worth living after God took my Anna."

"I like this quiet... it is restful," Katie replied as she smiled across the table at her new husband. "I suppose if I get lonesome I can always visit my folks, and I'll be glad to come back home."

Nick's heart jumped with joy as he noticed Katie's reference to home. Apparently she already considered this her home. He spoke, "Your mother made me promise that we would come over for dinner next Sunday. I think we will have plenty of opportunities to experience noise."

A few days later Katie' father, with Johann, Anna, and Peter, came knocking on their door. Katie hurried to add a little water to the left-over coffee and offered him a chair. He declined and said, "Mother wants me to take some of the spring wheat we harvested to Buller's mill. She wants some white bread to make some special *Tvaebuck* for Christmas. I have the younger children with me. While I wait for the miller to grind my wheat, we will gather more firewood." He turned to Nick, "I thought perhaps you would like to go along. Do you have enough wood to last through the winter? I have a feeling it might just snow anytime, and we had better be prepared."

Nick turned to Katie. "Would you like to go to your mother's while I go with Father?"

But Katie replied, "No, I had better not. I have dough started for *Tvaebuck* and I need to do some mending and cleaning. I think I should stay home."

In his heart again Nick was pleased to hear her reference to home. He was indeed pleased with his wife of just a few days. He had chosen wisely. God had taken, but God had also given. He was content.

Anna, Johann, and Peter greeted him cheerfully and together they set off. The ride to the mill was uneventful. There was not much of a road, and the wagon ruts were rough. Maybe proper roads would be built soon. Anna climbed onto Nick's lap. That was more comfortable than the hard boards of the wagon box.

When they got to the mill, there were already three others ahead of them, so they would have to wait for the milling. But right away they started chopping dead timber as the children picked up twigs and small branches.

It was late afternoon when they finally returned. Katie found the time to be very lonely, and she wished she had taken the dough and the mending to her mother's house, but now they were back and all was well. With this supply of wood they could weather any storm.

Chapter Twenty

The day after the trip to the mill, it started to snow, and soon the wind came up, too. It whistled around the soddy, and the newlyweds were indeed happy for the extra supply of wood. The skies were heavy and dark, and Nick could barely see to get to the stable end of the soddy. He carefully felt his way along the wall, milked the cow, and made sure the horses had enough hay. The well was too far from the house. He dared not venture that far for fear of getting lost, so he brought buckets of snow into the house to melt, both for the animals and for themselves. The supply of kerosene was running low, so they didn't light the lamp. They melted the snow on top of the stove and then let the fire burn low. To keep warm, they huddled together under the heavy wool comforters Anna had brought from the old country.

Nick cuddled his new wife and thanked God for her. If he had been alone, he could well have frozen to death, even in a soddy.

Activities in the community came to a standstill. Everyone was hunkered down trying to keep warm. Concern lest anyone might not have found shelter lurked in the back of each mind. They well remembered a year ago when the Quiring boys had been lost.

In the Epp household, the younger Hoinz was impatient. He wished to see his little Lena. He wondered if she were warm. He would have ventured out, but Father forbade it and refused to let him use the horses or even the oxen. He would just have to wait patiently. Young love needed to learn patience. He reminded Hoinz that hope deferred made it sweeter. During the few hours of daylight, the children played "Hide the Thimble," "I Spy," and other games the older siblings had taught them. The dim light was not enough to sew by or to read, even though the only book they had was the Holy Bible.

Three days of snow and blowing winds finally came to an end. The sun came out in a blaze, and the world was a winter wonderland. Johann and Peter immediately got their warm clothes on. They were going to go sledding. They were tired of having been cooped up so long. But after Hoinz and Cornelius came in from milking the cow and tending the other animals, they warned the children it was absolutely too cold to go sledding. They would simply have to wait a few days.

Abraham insisted on stepping out to see the new white landscape. He soon came back in all excited. "Father, our wheat field is just covered with geese. May I use the gun to shoot some?" Father was reluctant but agreed to go out with him. Bundled up with only their eyes and noses exposed, they ventured out together. They soon came back carrying as many as they could manage.

After removing some of their wraps, Father declared, "That field is covered with geese that have frozen. They evidently were grazing that wheat field when the storm hit. Here, Mother, is your new featherbed." And he handed her a frozen goose.

Soon the whole family was busy plucking the soft down. It was heavy, for nature had prepared the geese for a long winter, but not adequately enough for that severe cold spell. As the geese thawed out, they became more flexible, but the floor of the soddy was collecting snow, which was now melting, making it a slippery mess. The family continued to stuff the down into an empty pillowcase. When it would hold no more, Margaret got up to get another, but with the first step she slipped and ended up unceremoniously on her bottom on the messy floor. Fortunately, she was not hurt, just embarrassed. Her clothing, however, was sopping wet and muddy with the wet clay. She had to change, and Mother set about to get the mud out of her only everyday dress. Margaret huddled in her nightgown for the rest of the afternoon, while her dress hung from the ceiling to dry. After the plucking had been done, the geese were butchered. Three were cooked for supper, while the rest were packed in the snow bank behind the soddy.

The evening chores had to be done, so the older boys bundled up to feed the animals, milk the cow, and carry snow to be melted for the animals to drink. They brought in the milk and an extra bucket of snow to melt for household use. The water in the well had frozen, so they could not pump any.

Mother took some of the snow in her mixing bowl and stirred in some cream and a bit of molasses. Even though it was very cold, they enjoyed the new dessert mother had concocted.

The moon shone on that frozen area that night, and a few hours after the family had gone to bed, they were awakened by a deafening noise and commotion behind the soddy. Wolves were on the prowl and had discovered the cache of geese hidden in the snow bank. After appeasing their appetites, the wolves gathered in a circle and howled at the moon. Just before daylight they disappeared.

Meanwhile, at the Sperling household, Herman came in all excited. "I just found more than a dozen frozen prairie chickens. If I take them to Sutton, Mr. Copsey will give me ten cents apiece for them. That will be over a dollar." Herman had been taking prairie chickens to Mr. Copsey in Sutton periodically since early fall, where they were packed in a barrel covered with salt and shipped by train to Chicago and New York, where they were considered a real delicacy. But he had never had this many to sell at one time. "I can be back before dark if I hurry."

Mrs. Sperling agreed to let him go, but suggested he ask Abraham Epp to go with him. "And hurry, you never know when another snowstorm will blow in."

With his parents' approval, Abraham joined Herman, and they set off at a good pace. It was dusk when they returned disappointed. "Mr. Copsey wouldn't take them because he could not find evidence of them being shot. If they died of disease, they would be unfit to eat. How stupid! Surely he could tell they had frozen to death." With that he took his father's gun and shot each bird in the head. "In the morning I will take them again."

Mr. Copsey was happy to get them. "This will fill the barrel, and I can ship them this afternoon." He handed Herman a dollar and fifty cents, saying, "Good work my boy! I hope you can bring me more."

Mrs. Sperling was delighted to get the dollar and fifty cents. This would help to buy some dried fruit for the Christmas dinner.

After a few days, the weather again warmed up. The younger children enjoyed many hours sliding down the hills into the creek bottom. In the moonlight, some of the older children had some sledding parties as well.

Preparations were made for Christmas. Hoinz made good on his promise to build the traditional Christmas carousel, and they took it to the church for the Christmas Eve program. Everyone was cheerful. The snow would help the newly planted red winter wheat to stool out. They were optimistic for the crops next summer. On

sunny, moderate days, the men of the community would go either to
Sutton or Henderson for whatever was needed before the next storm
might come. Trips were often made to the mill at the river and, while
waiting for the wheat to be made into flour, twigs and other wood
was gathered to keep the home fires burning.

After a cold, snowy January and February, March came in like
a lamb. The children were able to go to school again after having
been deprived during the hard winter months. They were happy to
see their friends again and were eager to visit. The schoolmaster had
some trouble getting and keeping order. Abraham seemed to have
too much energy to sit still. He fidgeted and then pulled the pigtail
of Rachel Sperling, who sat in front of him. This caused her to turn
around and slap his face, which started a general commotion. Mr.
Wall tapped his desk loudly, and at last order was restored. Abraham
was ordered to stand in one corner and Rachel in another.

Later, as they all walked home together, Abraham begged his
siblings and Rachel not to tell the parents. He knew what would
happen if his father heard about the disturbance. He was sweet on
the Sperling girl, and she knew it. He didn't think she would tell, but
maybe her siblings would. At last, with some threatening of bodily
harm, everyone promised to keep the secret. But Abraham's sister
Margaret promised if he did it again, she would tell.

Toward the end of March, something else happened to close
the school for two weeks. The Kroeker children came down with
whooping cough. It soon spread to other families. In almost every
home, one or two children, and sometimes as many as three or four,
were affected. Anxiously, mothers hovered over their sick little ones.
They well remembered previous outbreaks of that dreaded disease
that had decimated families. They thought of the many little graves

they had left in the homeland and wondered how many new ones would be added here before this awful disease would run its course.

Mother Sperling watched over Esther, Alvin, and Daniel anxiously. Sometimes they would all go into a coughing spasm at the same time. Rachel and Thelma helped her as they patted the backs of those three to help them catch their breath. How relieved they were when at last the coughing stopped, but they knew it would come again. Little Daniel was the first; being just two, his little body could not fight this enemy. He was too young to take the medicine, which was a teaspoon of molasses with a drop of coal-oil in it. After sobbing bitterly for an hour, Catherine Sperling wrapped his little body in a blanket and had Herman lay it in the stable where it would stay cool. There was no time to plan a funeral. They were too busy with the other sick children. Two days later Esther succumbed to the malady, and a day later Alvin, too, died. Catherine Sperling had three little ones to add to that growing number of bodies in the cemetery behind the church. Would her sorrows never end? After sobbing despondently for almost an hour, she composed herself. The graves had to be dug, and caskets had to be built. She sent Herman to town to make the arrangements. Pastor Unruh, who was also good at woodworking, offered to make a casket. His wife would make a warm flannel lining. The children were small enough that one casket would do. It was a small funeral. Only the ones who had had the whooping cough were able to come, since they now had immunity. Pastor Unruh tried to preach a comforting sermon, but even his own voice broke now and then. A group of young people sang "Safe in the Arms of Jesus":

Children of the heavenly Father
Safely in His bosom gather;

Nestling bird nor star in heaven
Such a refuge e'er was given.
Though He giveth and He taketh,
God His children ne'er forsaketh;
His the loving purpose solely
To preserve them pure and holy.

There was much silent weeping in the congregation as the service ended with the congregation again singing, "Oh, they tell me of a home far away."

Many acts of kindness were offered to this poor widow, who had suffered so much. Other families, too, suffered loss. The Epps buried Peter and little Anna. Jake and his new wife, Elizabeth, buried little three-year-old Peter. The community mourned, but understood that life must go on.

Eventually the disease ran its course, and normal activities were resumed. The school closed for the summer season. Everyone was needed to do the farm and garden work.

Chapter Twenty-One

It was a prosperous year. The precious red winter wheat produced abundantly, as did the oats, barley, and rye. Hoinz bought a sow that was due to have piglets any day. After the piglets were weaned, the sow would be butchered for the winter meat supply. The family needed the lard as much as anything.

Farmers were looking for more land to develop. Most farmsteads now had grain storage sheds built of lumber purchased at Henry Kroeker's lumberyard in Henderson. Every farmstead had also added some livestock. They now would have milk for their households. The baked goods tasted so much better made with milk, or even cream, instead of water. And it was a luxury to have eggs in abundance, as well chickens for Sunday dinner. They would not have to depend on wild animals for their supply of meat. Makeshift buildings had been constructed to protect these animals from prowling predators. Wolves howled at night, but they could not touch the chickens, ducks, geese, and piglets safely housed in these hastily built shanties.

But most of the families still lived in soddies. How Katharina wished she could have a real house for her family to live in, but she dared not mention it to Hoinz. The other structures were more important, and she was thankful that they were now assured that their own food supply would last through the coming winter. The soddy was warm and not nearly as crowded as it had been at the beginning. Nick Thiezen had moved out, as had Katie, when she and Nick were married, and Hoinz by now had his own place with his wife Lena. And of course little Anna and Peter were gone. They had plenty of room, but she missed her little ones terribly. Although Nick and Katie and Hoinz and Lena usually came for Sunday dinner, the house seemed empty with so many gone. How she missed little Anna and Peter. She also thought often of the two little graves they had left in Russia. Life was hard. There was so much sorrow in the world. Sometimes she thought she just couldn't bear it any longer, but then she would think of Catherine Sperling, who had had a far greater loss. She would manage to do some extra baking and take it over to her friend Catherine. And after a little visit she was encouraged. Mrs. Sperling seemed to be an inspiration to so many people. She always reminded everyone about that home faraway. These troubles and sorrows were only temporary.

On this particular day, Katharina walked home to find that Hoinz was back from town with the wagon filled with lumber. What was he going to build now?

"Katharina, come look what I have brought. Since the winter wheat has been planted and the plowing is done, I thought it was time we did something to the house. We will build a floor and plaster the walls. That will make the house more pleasant and comfortable for you this winter. If we have a good crop next year, we will put lumber around the outside, and your house will be as grand as any in the town of Henderson."

There was much sawing and pounding for the next two weeks. Fortunately, most of the sawing could be done outside, but the little furniture they had had to be moved from one side to another as the floor was put in place. And then it had to be moved again, as the two-by-fours were put up so the lath, which would hold the plaster, could be nailed in place.

Mr. Quiring came to do the plastering, and after a month of disorder, they had a truly lovely home.

Winter came with Christmas merrymaking, according to tradition. Mothers were filled with anxiety, wondering what illness might take members of the family this year. The whooping cough of the year before still lingered in their minds. They tucked their little ones in carefully each night, realizing the frailty of those little lives.

There was no major outbreak of disease that winter, but Albert Fast complained of a growing sore throat when he came home from school one day in February. His mother, Elizabeth, tucked him into bed immediately. She remembered how her brother had come down with a sore throat back in Russia six years before. He had died four days later of diphtheria. She placed a mustard plaster on Albert's chest. He went to sleep almost immediately, and she went to prepare supper for her family. When she checked on him later that evening, she found he had a high fever. She urged him to drink a little warm water, but he refused it, saying his throat hurt so badly that he could not swallow. Jake came to help, and they bathed his face and body with cool water.

After a few minutes, he spoke to his mother with great difficulty. "When Papa died, you said he went to be with Jesus. If I die, will I go to be with Jesus, too?"

Shocked to hear these words from her son, Elizabeth broke into tears. Jake took over, "What is it, son?"

And again the boy spoke brokenly, "Will I go to be with Papa and Jesus, or will I go to that other place Pastor Unruh spoke about?"

Jake remembered that Pastor Unruh was honest about what the scripture said about both heaven and hell. He didn't realize that this dear boy was concerned about this. They needed to explain to their children that those who trusted in Jesus would definitely go to be with Jesus. So, with a trembling voice, he spoke to this child he claimed as his own. "You know that Jesus died on the cross and that He rose again and went to heaven. Do you know that He died for you, for all the wrong things you have ever done? You know that everybody does wrong sometimes."

"Like the time I pulled Martha's hair and the time I took Matilda's candy?"

"Yes, and the time you talked back to your mother. Just tell Jesus you are sorry, that you want Him to come into your heart and take away all the bad things. He will do that, and then you will know for sure that you will go to be with Jesus. But I don't want you to go for a long time. I want you to get well and help me drive those horses, and we want to go sledding and do many things for fun before the spring work begins."

"Okay, Papa," he whispered, and he went back to sleep.

Anxiously Jake and Elizabeth watched over his bed, making sure the other children stayed their distance, lest this might be catching.

Albert seemed a little better in the morning. He managed to swallow a little bit of water with molasses, but as a precaution, Jake suggested he take the other children to the grandparents for a few days. That way Elizabeth would have time to care for Albert without interruptions.

The children were happy to spend some time at Grandma's. Maybe she would have some molasses cookies for them. Elizabeth would not let them near Albert's bed, so they called their goodbyes from a safe distance. Jake bundled them up and loaded them into the wagon that now had runners instead of wheels, and they were off to Grandmother's house.

As soon as they left, Albert motioned for his mother to come close. In a low whisper he told her that he had asked Jesus to come into his heart, and he was not afraid of that other place now. He knew he would go to be with Jesus and his papa.

Elizabeth had trouble controlling her emotions but said, "I am glad you did that, Albert, but please don't go for a long time."

"Maybe when I get as old as Grandpa, I'll go. First I have to help my new papa with the horses."

Tearfully, Elizabeth bathed his feverish body again, and he went to sleep. Eagerly she waited for the return of her husband. She had words of comfort for him, but her heart was also full of anxiety. She prayed.

A week later another burial was held at the growing cemetery. Only the pastor and Jake and Elizabeth were there. The danger of this contagious disease was too great for others to attend. The doctor had told of one child in Sutton who had died of the disease that winter, but spring had come with no other outbreaks. For that they were thankful. Martha, Matilda, and Mary came back home a week later, and the house was again filled with some laughter and childish chatter, but there were outbreaks of tears, too. First, Peter with the whooping cough, and now Albert, with the dreaded diphtheria.

Jake realized that with the joy of having a wife and family came sorrow and tears as well.

Spring came with all the work of planting fields and gardens. Martha offered to help Jake with the field work since Albert was gone. She learned to handle the horses quite well and beamed when Jake praised her at the supper table. Matilda wanted to help as well, but Elizabeth insisted she needed her in the house and the garden.

Everyone was busy. It helped to keep their minds off the loss they had experienced, but nevertheless, there were times when tears were shed in secret.

And then in July Elizabeth found that she was with child. Oh, how happy she was. She just hoped she could give Jake a son. It would please him so much. He had been so kind to take her and the five children, and he treated those little ones as though they were his very own. She kept her secret for some time, until at last Jake questioned her about it as they lay in bed discussing the work that needed to be done the next day. When she confirmed his suspicions, he held her close and whispered, "I am delighted. I love my girls, but I sure would like to have a boy. I just don't understand why God should choose to take both of our boys."

Elizabeth noted the reference to "our" boys, and it filled her with contentment. The Lord had taken Johann from her, but He had given her a good man. She snuggled in his arms and went to sleep.

Chapter Twenty-Two

After the planting was done that May, there was a lull in the activities of the farm, and with the daylight lasting longer, families took time to visit their neighbors. One night the Isaac Penner family came to see the Epps. The children played outside. Even the parents brought out chairs to visit in the shade of the soddy. Mrs. Epp proudly showed Mrs. Penner her two lilac bushes, laden with buds. She would have lilacs in a few days. Katharina already smelled the flowers in her mind. Mrs. Penner spoke of her yard. She was happy to have some bushes, too, and thought that her peonies would do well. The trees that had been painstakingly transplanted from the Blue River area had taken root, and although it would take a few more years before the settlers could sit in the shade, it was good to see them growing. The elder Hoinz and Isaac walked to the nearby wheat field. The shafts were now almost a foot high. Hopes were high for a good crop in a few more months.

As the sun set and it began to grow dark, the Penners left.

The next day Father called Maria to help him with the fence he had built around the chicken house. She wondered if there was some special reason for this seemingly unnecessary errand. She soon found out.

"Maria," her father said as soon as they were far enough away from the house to not be heard. "That Penner boy is a fine young man. He is a hard worker. The Penners are successful farmers, well respected in the community. Young Frank has shown an interest in you, yet it seems you ignore him, and at times you seem to be actually rude to the young man. I suggest you change your attitude toward him. His parents are hoping to turn the farm over to him in the next few years. It is right next to ours and would make it easy for us to work together. You are eighteen now. It is time you thought of marriage. Cornelius will soon be ready to take over our place in a few years, and Mother and I will also move to town. I don't see anyone better than young Frank coming along, do you?"

Maria tried not to show her dismay; after all, this was her father speaking. *Was he actually picking a husband for her? That was so archaic! Didn't young people make their own choices in this day and age? Hadn't her brother Hoinz fallen in love with Lena Franz? That's why he had married her. Didn't Katie marry Nick Thiezen because she loved him? And what about Jake Sperling? Wasn't it love that brought him and Elizabeth Fast together?* This was her father. How could she answer him? She could not disagree with him; that wasn't allowed. *But, Frankie Penner!?* She would rather be an old maid than to be tied to that pompous idiot. For a long time she said nothing. She continued to help her father stretch the wire so the chickens would not escape.

Finally Father said, "Well, Maria, what do you say to this?"

Maria mumbled almost inaudibly, "I will think about it."

"Very good," replied her father. "I'm sure you will see this is good for all involved." And he dismissed her to go back to helping her mother in the garden.

Maria was panic-stricken. What would she do? How she wished she could talk to her sister Sarah, but Sarah was so far away, and Maria did not dare to put her thoughts in a letter. She finally resolved that she would talk to her sister Katie. There had to be some way to get out of this. She reached into her pocket and rubbed the little bird she had carried there for almost three years now. Where was Karl Regier? Had he forgotten her? Was he married to some other girl in Russia and intending to stay there? Her thoughts tormented her late into the night. She must go see Katie tomorrow. She could not talk to her mother about this, for Father's word was law, and Mother knew it.

Katie was happy to see Maria, and they conversed happily as Maria helped her weed the large garden behind the house.

Maria debated with herself as to how she should approach the subject that so troubled her. After a long silence, Katie looked at her sister and said, "Now, Maria, I know you had a special reason for coming over here. It is not because you just like to pull weeds."

Biting her lip to keep back the tears, Maria blurted out, "Do you love Nick? Or did Father arrange for you to marry him?"

"Oh, my dear little sister, of course I love Nick, more every day. He is a good man. But why did you even ask such a silly question? I am sure he loves me, too; not like he loved Anna, as she was his first love. Since he lost Anna, I think he values me even more."

"Father wants me to marry Frankie Penner, and I don't like him at all."

Katie paused and then said softly, "There are several marriages in the community that are marriages of convenience, or you might say, of necessity. Some of the individuals learn to love each other, while others simply tolerate each other. But they respect each other and make a home for the children involved. Maybe you could learn to love Frankie, or at least respect him. He would provide you with a fine house."

"I don't want a fine house. I just want someone to love me and not simply think of me as a boost to his success."

"If you feel that strongly, maybe I can have Nick talk to Father. Father thinks well of Nick, and I am sure he was pleased that the two of us got married. Maybe he will listen to Nick. I can see you are in a fix that I cannot fix." And she laughed at her own clever statement.

Maria smiled but could not laugh. She was simply too upset. After a little more conversation, Maria returned home. She felt a bit of relief for having shared her problem with Katie. But she could not see a solution and continued to be despondent.

A week later a traumatic event almost changed Maria's mind. The day had started unusually warm, even for late May. Clouds began to build all around – dark, ominous clouds. They grew darker and higher, especially in the Northwest and the Southeast. Father, Cornelius, and Abraham came in from the field. They turned the horses loose and hurried into the house. This was most unusual. They never quit before dark or the raindrops started falling. Father gathered the family around and said, "This looks like a really big storm. I hope we don't get hail. That could destroy all our hopes of a crop." Occasionally he stepped to the door to check the situation, only to report it was getting darker. There was no wind, and it was beastly hot. Then suddenly the wind picked up and increased in ferocity. Soon it fairly rattled the windows and doors. And then the rain started. It pounded the roof and then became even louder. That was hail! They had never heard the noise of the wind and rain to this degree before. What could be happening? Mother wondered what was happening to the garden and their crops as well as their animals. Father was going to go out to check on the animals, but this time Mother angrily forbade him. And he listened to her. *It must be really bad*, thought Maria. Father never listened to Mother. It got so dark Mother felt around to find the lamp, and Father found matches to light it. They huddled around the table wondering if the roof would be lifted off their heads. Father held his head in despair. Was all his labor to be in vain?

Then suddenly it was quiet. The rain continued, but the hail had apparently stopped, and the wind was almost calm. After another few minutes, even the rain stopped. Soon the sun came out, and a brilliant rainbow appeared in the eastern sky. Father and the boys took off their shoes to go out and check out the damage. The animals were secure in the barn. The chickens came out bewildered. This was a new day for them, as they had gone to roost because of the darkness. Father and the boys checked the garden, which looked like a total loss. The fields near the house were flattened by the hail. They must check on their neighbors. Mrs. Sperling and her family were fine. She invited them in for coffee, commenting she had thought sure they were headed for "that home faraway." But she was glad they had been spared and that her neighbors, too, were safe.

Hoinz and his boys returned to their own home relieved that the Sperlings were spared. Their feet were blue with cold since they had walked through hail and cold water and mud. They warmed themselves and got their stockings and shoes back on. They would take the horses to check on neighbors farther away.   As Father rode toward Nick and Katie's house, he sent Cornelius to check on the Penners. What Cornelius found at the Penners caused him to turn his horse and gallop back to catch his father. "Oh, you must come quickly. The Penners' house is totally gone." Hoinz joined his son and together they rode back to the Penner homestead. They found

Mr. Penner wandering around, his left arm dangling at his side and his right hand at his head.

Father called to him as Mr. Penner walked toward them. "Everything is gone!" he wailed, "everything I worked so hard for. My wife is in the hay wagon over there. She is dead! I tried to pick her up, but this arm won't work. I cannot find my children. Frank was holding the door for me. I had gone to close the barn door. I was almost there when everything turned black. I am looking for Frank and Barbara and Jacob. Can you help me find them?"

Immediately Hoinz and Cornelius joined the search. They soon found Barbara beside the binder. She was covered with mud and unconscious. Cornelius was ordered to take her to the Epp house to be cleaned up.

By now other neighbors had arrived, and the search continued. After some time, they found Jacob wedged between two barrels. He, too, was unconscious and covered with mud.

Mother and Maria carefully removed the remnants of Barbara's clothes and tenderly washed her. They had just finished when they heard a deep sigh, and Barbara was gone. But now the men arrived with Mr. Penner and Jacob, and the work started all over. Mr. Epp and Cornelius stayed to clean them up.

Where, oh where, would they find Frank? Maria felt remorseful and prayed that she would be forgiven for those bad feelings she had had for him. She even considered changing her attitude if only he could be found. Two hours later, word came that he had been found a half mile down the creek, still holding on to the door waiting for his father to enter. He had been taken to the Quirings' house to be cleaned up and cared for.

Again caskets were made, and the funeral for Mrs. Penner and her daughter was planned.

But the Quirings had had enough. Although their house was spared, their crops were totally destroyed. They were going back to Russia. And although others tried to dissuade them, they remained firm. They had lost two boys in the blizzard two years ago, and now this. They were determined. They offered their house to Isaac Penner and began immediately to pack up their personal belongings. They had had enough of this "land of promise."

The community came together to mourn this devastating loss. How quickly things could change from joy and gladness to sorrow and suffering!

But time goes on, and time eases the blow of tragedy. After a year of rebuilding, Isaac Penner married a widow with two children. Frank never fully recovered from the trauma of the tornado, but he was able to persuade his stepsister to marry him, and they continued to farm in the area.

Chapter Twenty-Three

After having had such high hopes for a bountiful harvest, the settlers were thankful that the crops were not a total ruin. Most farmers realized about half of what they had expected, and there was always the hope of next year.

There was great news at the church picnic. Pastor Unruh had received notice that another group of Russian Mennonites were on their way to settle in Nebraska. The Russian government was continuing its harassment of the Mennonites because of their objection to military service. The Mennonites could no longer tolerate the pressure from the Russian government, so they were seeking to join the earlier settlers in the Henderson area. Despite the red tape involved in getting exit visas, they were finally on their way and expected to arrive in Henderson sometime in the middle of August. Pastor Unruh had a list of those expecting to come.

The congregation listened intently as he read the list. Everybody was eager to see if relatives were on the list. It would be wonderful to reunite with those to whom they had sorrowfully bid farewell years ago. Katharina wiped tears of joy from her eyes, and Hoinz blinked to keep his own tears from rolling down his cheeks.

Sarah and Peter Weins were on the list, along with Peter and Anna Weins. *They must have two children. How exciting!* thought Katharina.

Maria listened intently, but she did not hear the name Regier. She was disappointed, but she hid her disappointment from all those around her. Apparently Karl had forgotten her and married someone else.

At the Sunday School picnic two weeks later, Elizabeth sought out Katie Thiezen and confidentially told her friend her secret. Katie clasped her friend's hand and confided that she, too, was with child to be born in October. She asked Elizabeth to pray for her husband Nick, as he was extremely worried that this would end as it had with Anna on board the ship. "He hovers over me all the time, even when I assure him everything is going well. I keep telling him that my mother bore all those children without a problem. I am built just like my mother and will probably give birth to a dozen healthy babies."

To which Elizabeth replied, "Not all at once I hope!" They both laughed heartily at that and then joined the other women setting out the picnic food.

When August arrived, everyone was eagerly waiting further word as to when the new settlers would arrive. And when the word came, those expecting relatives went to the railroad station to welcome them and take them into their homes until housing could be provided. The whole Epp family stood waiting eagerly for the train to arrive. When it finally chugged into the station and released a cloud of steam, a great cheer arose. Families that had been parted for three years were reunited with hugs and tears. Even some of the most hardened stoics wiped their eyes.

Maria welcomed her sister Sarah and her family, but her eyes kept scanning the crowd. Even though his name was not on the list, she was hoping against hope that Karl would be there. And then she saw him. Leaving all semblance of decorum behind, she rushed to him. He saw her at about the same time and they met. With total disregard for what people might think, they hugged right there in public.

Since she was again working for Mrs. Kroeker, Maria did not need to go home with her family. Discreetly she returned to where her family was gathering the belongings of the new arrivals. She hugged her sister and the two little ones again and then announced that she needed to return to work. She would see them on Sunday.

She would walk to the Kroeker house. Perhaps she could persuade Mrs. Kroeker to offer shelter to Karl, who had come alone. Karl would follow her at some distance to see how this would work out. Mrs. Kroeker was more than happy to welcome Karl. Although she had not said anything to Maria, she disapproved of Mr. Epp's harshness with his children and especially of the way he demanded the money that Maria earned. She had on occasion slipped an extra dollar into Maria's pocket and said, "This is not part of your pay; this is just for you."

The Kroekers were eager to hear about all that was going on in their old homeland and about the trip, but at last they left Maria and Karl alone in the parlor while they returned to the kitchen.

Karl feasted his eyes on Maria, and for a minute neither spoke. Then Maria reached into her pocket and pulled out the little wooden bird. "See? I have kept this all this time, hoping you would come to Nebraska. Did your parents allow you to come, or did you sneak away?"

"I pestered them to the point of them letting me go. They were not happy about it, but here I am!" and then he withdrew a folded paper from his pocket. Unfolding it he revealed that bit of hair she had given him. The paper showed a drawing, somewhat faded, but still clear enough to be recognized. It was a drawing of Maria's likeness. "I'm not much of an artist, but I drew this the day you left. I have kept it with me all this time hoping I would see you again." After a little more conversation, they rejoined those in the kitchen, and Mr. Kroeker showed Karl a space in the attic of the carriage house where he could stay until he could find better living quarters.

Karl was delighted and offered thanks. This was much better than he had hoped, for he would be close to Maria, and tomorrow he would find a job.

The state of Nebraska was thriving in spite of setbacks caused by weather and disease. The population was increasing every year as immigrants came from all over Europe. There was a need for roads to replace the wagon trails that led from one homestead to another. New courthouses also needed to be built in both York and Hamilton Counties. So Karl, along with many others, found gainful employment immediately. Although the settlers expressed some dismay that the wagon trails were not going to be developed, they were happy to be offered the opportunity to work on the roads that were to be built along the surveyed mile markers.

And another winter passed. Again the crops looked promising, but the farmers were not counting their prosperity until the grain was in the bin. They had learned the hard way.

Mr. Klippenstein had heard of various new farm implements coming out of Chicago. He had sold many horse-pulled mowers. Very few farmers used a scythe anymore. Now he heard about a machine that would cut grain and tie it into bundles automatically. He wanted to see one in operation. A few weeks later, he got a flier picturing this contraption in his mail. It sure did look complicated. Along with the mailing was an invitation to see it demonstrated within the next week.

He could hardly wait for twelve o'clock so he could go home and tell his wife about it. Finally, he told his son Aaron to take charge of the store. He was going home early.

His wife was surprised to see him at eleven. He never showed up until twelve or later. His lunch was not ready.

"Don't worry about lunch! I am too excited to eat," he said as he showed her the picture with the invitation. "I am going to take the train to see this thing. If it works like they say it does, every farmer will want one. It will save them so much time and hard labor."

His wife was a little dubious. She commented, "With all the modern contraptions, the farmers will get lazy. But if it works, it will be a good thing." She went on, "I suppose one day someone will come up with a contraption that will cut the grain, thresh, it and put it into the granary without the farmer touching it. Then the young men and the women who earn a few pennies shocking the bundles will be loafing in town, but they won't have work, so they won't have money to spend."

"It just might happen! So many new things are coming on the market. Just look at your washing machine with a wringer. Nobody uses a wash board anymore. By the way, would you like to go to Chicago with me next week?"

Seldom did people take the train to go farther than York or Lincoln, but the next week Mr. and Mrs. Klippenstein were waiting at the station for the train to Chicago. This was such an occasion that several townspeople came to the station to see them off.

A week later they were back, and Mr. Klippenstein invited the farmers of the area to witness a demonstration to be held at the Epp's farm. Mr. Epp's grain was ready to be cut, and he had offered the implement dealer the opportunity to demonstrate the new-fangled equipment. Hopefully the reaper would arrive in time. A crowd gathered quickly at the Epp farm. Even wives came with their children. Everyone was eager to see this, but most were skeptical. Would it work?

Mr. Klippenstein rented some horses at the livery barn and started for the Epp farm. The horses were skeptical as well and threatened to bolt as they were hitched to this strange-looking contraption. They had never been required to pull anything other than wagons. At last the hitching was done, and they started for the farm. The first turn around the field was a disaster. The twine that was to tie the bundles kept breaking. But with a few adjustments, it finally did what it was supposed to do, and the people cheered. Mr. Klippenstein had a special deal with the McCormick Deering Company, allowing the farmers to order the machine and pay for it after the harvest. Mr. Klippenstein took orders for six of the machines that day. They would come on the train next week, just in time for the harvesting. Fathers and sons shared the machine, and those who didn't have sons partnered with neighbors, for the machine was too expensive for one man to buy. The risk of it not working was too great.

That Sunday the congregation noticed Mrs. Klippenstein wearing a new hat. The congregation thought, "Ah, such vanity!" But it wasn't long until a few others visited the Ratzloff Mercantile looking for new bonnets as well.

Dutifully Maria went home every Sunday. It was good to see her family, and when Nick and Katie showed up with a healthy baby boy in October, there was even greater rejoicing. The house was again filled with noise. Mrs. Epp was happy with her soddy, now that the inside was finished with plaster. The outside would have to wait another year, but that didn't matter. Father had not mentioned Frank Penner to Maria again. After the tornado, Frank had become listless, lacking ambition, and so no longer offered such prosperity to the family.

Hoinz knew that Karl Regier had arrived and was living with the Kroekers, but nothing was said about it. Maria's mother had not mentioned Karl to her, either. Katie and Sarah asked about him occasionally, and Maria would only reply that she hardly saw him, since he was working early and late on the county road project. She did not tell them that she was making lunch daily for him to take to work.

When Christmas drew near, Maria gathered her courage and asked her father if she could bring Karl to the family dinner. He answered without enthusiasm, "Whatever your mother says about it is okay."

Mother agreed to Maria's planned invitation. She was happy that the situation with the Penner boy had reversed itself. She did want her daughters to have happy marriages. Life had enough troubles without the hardship of living with a man for whom and from whom there was no love.

At first the conversation was a bit strained at the Christmas gathering, but soon the men were asking about the progress of the road construction and how soon it would be completed. Father asked pointedly, "And what will you be doing when the roads are finished?"

Karl replied courteously, "The superintendent has offered me a job of maintaining the roads. They will need continual smoothing after rainstorms, when they will develop deep ruts, and they will need plowing after snowstorms. I will have the job to maintain the roads around the area of Henderson. I have talked to Mr. Ratzloff about buying the house his parents lived in. Since old Mrs. Ratzloff died, Mr. Ratzloff has been living with each of his children, six weeks at a time. I don't want to wear out my welcome at the Kroekers'. They have been so good to me."

Chapter Twenty-Four

When Karl and Maria drove back to the Kroeker house that night in the buggy he had rented at the livery barn, Karl asked if Maria had heard the conversation with her father. She admitted that she had tried to listen to it, but with all the other chatter at the table, she had heard only bits and pieces of their conversation. So Karl filled her in with the promise of the permanent job offer, as well as his plans to buy the house vacated by the elder Ratzloffs. Then he turned to her and said softly, "I want you to live in that house with me. It is not fancy, and it is very small, but we can manage. And when our babies come along, we can add to it. I'm asking you to marry me as soon as the road work is done and I start that regular job." Then he put his arm around her shoulders, and, drawing her close, added, "Please say yes!"

Maria blushed as she looked him in the eye. "How could I say no, when this is what I have wanted since the day you gave me this little bird? When we are settled in that little house, I will place it on the china cupboard, and there it will remain. I won't need to keep it in my pocket any longer."

This time Karl gave her an emphatic kiss on the lips and promised many more of the same.

The winter passed all too slowly for the newly engaged couple. Father had given his approval, although reluctantly. In his view, any man who didn't own land or farm it wasn't worth his salt.

The wedding came at the end of March, just before the farmers again started the planting season. Maria would wear the same dress that her mother, Sarah, and Katie had worn. A few alterations were again made. This time the church had an organ and an organist who played music while the bride and groom made their way down the center aisle of the church. Well-wishers brought useful household gifts. The *Tvaebuck*, sausage, and *Plautz* were enjoyed by the guests with adequate amounts of coffee and real cream and white sugar cubes. Karl and Maria piled the gifts behind the seat of a newly purchased buggy with a spirited horse to pull it. They drove off to Elm Street, where the little house awaited them. They were together and never would they part.

This year there were few spring storms, and the crops looked healthy. Again they were hopeful for a harvest, but this time their anticipation was not as great. They well knew all the things that could happen between planting and harvest. But the harvesting went well and much more quickly with the new binders. The grain bins were bulging with the crops. Kroeker Grain Company was impatient for train cars to arrive so the crops could be shipped to Omaha, Minneapolis, and Chicago. Klippenstein took orders for more reapers in time for the next year's crop.

The storm came about a week after the grain harvest was finished. The sky turned black in mid-afternoon, and the wind came up as well. This time there was no tornado, but the rain intensified, and soon hail joined in and pounded through the night and the next day. The creek rose higher and higher. Hoinz and Katharina were concerned about their neighbor on the other side of the creek, but there was no way to check on her. They could not cross that roaring, rushing water.

But as always, the rain did eventually stop, and people everywhere stepped out to see what damage had been done. Fortunately, the grain had been harvested. Even if they lost the corn crop, they would survive. Hoinz and Katharina stepped out and looked across the way. All they could see was water. The swollen creek covered the opposite bank and spread far into the field on the other side. *What had happened to Mrs. Sperling and her family?*

The water receded in about a week, but there was no sign of the dugout where Mrs. Sperling had lived so contentedly. Jake came riding up to the Epp house as soon as the storm-swollen creek allowed. What had been a lazy, meandering creek running gently past his mother's front door was now a scene of devastation. Katharina met him at the door.

"Have you seen my mother?" he asked, hoping they had taken her in before the creek rose so high.

Katharina had to explain the obvious: that Mrs. Sperling and the children were gone.

Jake explained that Tina and Rachel were safe in Henderson, where they had jobs at the hotel. Willie was at Jake and Elizabeth's house. Jake's mother had been home alone.

Brokenhearted, Jake left to inform his sisters and his little brother of the obvious fate of their mother.

After a week the creek waters receded, and an intensive search was made for Mrs. Sperling's body. It was found, caught in some tree roots, just before the creek emptied into the Blue River.

Another funeral was held, this one well attended; everyone who had known Mrs. Sperling loved her courage and fortitude.

Chapter Twenty-Four

The congregation sang:

O they tell me of a home far beyond the skies,
O they tell me of a home far away;
O they tell me of a home where no storm clouds rise,
O they tell me of an unclouded day.
O they tell me of a home where my friends have gone,
O they tell me of a land far away,
Where the tree of life in eternal bloom
Sheds its fragrance thro' the unclouded day,
O they tell me that He smiles on His children there,
And His smile drives their sorrows all away,
And they tell me that no tears ever come again
In that land of the unclouded day.
O the land of cloudless day,
O the land of an unclouded day;
O they tell me of a home where no storm clouds rise,
O they tell me of an unclouded day.

Beloved Mrs. Sperling had found the place she could call home.

Glossary

The Mennonites who emigrated from Russia to Nebraska in the late 1800's spoke a dialect of Low German. Many words in this dialect were similar to Yiddish. When two entries are listed in this glossary, the first is an approximation of the Low German word remembered by the author. The second entry is a more traditional German word or phrase.

Faspa or *Abendessen* – a special afternoon lunch or supper

Fröliche Weihnachten – Merry Christmas

Gott ist die Liebe – God is love

Guten Tag – good day

Kaiskie Kruit – a round-leafed weed with a tiny seed encased in a green husk

Kielkes – homemade noodles

Kleitaschope or *Kleiderschrank* – wardrobe

Kumst Borscht or *Kohlsuppe* – beet soup or cabbage soup

mein Liebchen – my little one

Mos or *Mus* – soup made by cooking the weed with white sauce

Neeyoish Kuka or *Neujahrskekse* – New Year's cookies

O, Du Sehlige, O, Du Fröliche – Oh, Thou Holy One; Oh, Thou Joyful One

O, Vienass Boem, O Vienass Boem, wie grün sind deine Blätter! or *O Tannenbaum, O Tannenbaum, wie grün sind deine Blätter!* – Oh, Christmas Tree, Oh, Christmas Tree: How very green your leaves!

Paepa Naeta or *Pfeffernüsse* – peppernuts, small spicy cookies

Paipa Kraut or *Pfefferkraut* – pepperweed

Perieschkje or *Apfelstrudel* – a square pastry filled with cut up apples and sugar

Plautz – a type of pastry

Plumamos or *Plumenmoos* – fruit soup

Ruggabrot or *Roggenbrot* – rye bread

Schinken Fleisch or *Schinken* – ham

Snetya – another type of pastry

So nim den meine hendie, und fiedich mich, or *So nehme meine Hände und liefer mich aus* – So take Thou my hand and deliver me

Stille Nacht, Heilige Nacht – Silent Night, Holy Night

Tvaebuck or *Broodjes* – bread rolls

Verenika or *Käsetaschen* – a pastry filled with cottage cheese

Voah vie daught mocha? or *Werden wir dat henkriege?* – Will we make it?

Wenn Gott es will or *Vun Gott vilt* – If God wills

Zucker Kuka or *Plätzchen* – sugar cookies

Notes from the author

This is a fictional account of the Mennonites who migrated from Russia to Henderson in 1874. I hope you enjoyed reading it. My great-grandparents were a part of that group. In writing this, I was tempted to romanticize the story and make it more "lovey-dovey," but I made the difficult decision to tell it the way it really was.

They say truth is stranger than fiction. I think you will agree. Though this account is fictionalized, some of the people in this story really existed, and some of the events really happened.

Mr. Johann Fast (his real name) died the day before they were to leave Russia. His wife Elizabeth Fast (also her real name) left Russia with their five children. The oldest was eight; the youngest, two months. She kept her reservation for the voyage to America on the day after his death, knowing that her husband would be properly buried by the church people of the community in Russia.

Mrs. Catherine Sperling's (her real name) husband died on the train in the vicinity of Berlin on the way to the seaport at Hamburg. She feared there would be delays if this became known, so she kept his death a secret until the train arrived in to Hamburg. Since this was a violation of the rules, she had to pay a hefty fine. The group did have enough time in Hamburg to hold a proper funeral for him. Mrs. Sperling continued the journey to America with nine children, aged five months to 24 years. The part about her death in this book is fictional. It is true that there were dugouts washed out in cloudbursts, but it is not known if Mrs. Sperling's was one of them.

The incident about the prairie chickens is also true, although it did not involve a Mennonite boy. When I heard this account, I just thought it was too good to leave out.

The incident of the tornado is also true, although it actually happened in 1890, not in 1874 as depicted in this story. The names of the people and how and where they were found after this natural disaster are factual. I believe I knew the great-grandson of Isaac Penner. His name was Franz. I overheard adults talking about this tornado when I was a child in the early 1930's.

These people were very devout and steadfast in their belief that Christians should not serve in the military; however, they were not all that pacifist in other matters. They did not believe in frivolities. Although they firmly believed that salvation came by faith in Jesus Christ's death and resurrection, they thought being solemn and plain gave them favor with God.

Fathers felt God had ordained them to be heads of the household, and they ruled with an iron fist in most places. They believed children were an asset, as they would help with the never-ending manual work that was required before the age of modern machinery. They believed in that "Home Far Away" and did not expect any luxuries before they got there.

As Mrs. Sperling once said, "Men love their land, their wives, and their children, in that order." Public displays of affection were frowned upon, and a show of emotion was a sign of weakness or a lack of faith.

Apart from family lore, much of my information came from the Henderson Centennial book *From Holland to Henderson*, which I used with permission from the Henderson Historical Society.

Marion Siebert Jensen, 2016

CPSIA information can be obtained
at www.ICGtesting.com
Printed in the USA
BVHW040923010319
541542BV00015B/103/P